DEMON BOUND

THE CAMELOT ARCHIVE - BOOK ONE

NICOLE R. TAYLOR

1

———

*M*adeleine Greenbriar, what have you gotten yourself into this time?

The lingering scent of sulphur tickled my nostrils as I walked down the dark street, the trail leading me towards Islington High Street.

Dammit, it was trying to hide.

I could hear the throb of heavy music before I turned the corner and my heart sank and rose, if such a thing was possible.

The line for the nightclub snaked down the block, humans dressed in their best outfits. Death-rockers, punks, and goths huddled in their cliques as they waited to get inside London's longest running alternative venue, *Adrenaline*.

Mohawks, tattoos, and piercings were the flavour of the subculture, along with corsets, buckles, and elaborate hair extensions. There were a few futuristic looks—android-esque with plastic tubing hair and spiked welding goggles—and others wore more

traditional goth attire made up of lace and velvet…
and then there was me.

I had the all black thing down pat, but my
profession demanded I paired the colour with tactical
gear. Trousers with pockets, an arondight blade—a
magical blade that retracted into its hilt—at my left
hip, a cold iron dagger made from a meteorite on my
right, and another in my combat boot. The rest of the
uniform was a simple tight black T-shirt and a leather
jacket. The last bit was an amendment on my part.
My last shred off rebelliousness now that I was a full-
fledged Natural warrior. At least my hair was
naturally dark.

I scanned the crowd, my senses coming up blank.
My target wasn't out here.

I walked past the line of humans, my boots
thudding against the uneven concrete. The security
guards checking ID didn't bother to lift their heads as
I passed, but they wouldn't have seen me even if they
did. The first rule of patrolling was to remain
concealed at all times.

I was a Natural—a demon-hunting mage—born
to fight the Darkness from beyond the rift. Even
though the rift was closed five years ago, it didn't
mean we ridded the world of the demons who sought
to consume it. We'd gone from soldiers in a war to the
cleanup crew. It wasn't the kind of hero I wanted to
be, but after I'd almost become a casualty of said war
before I'd even graduated from the Academy, I
supposed manning a mop wasn't all that bad.

That's how I found myself on the hunt at a goth

club, of all places. I wasn't supposed to be patrolling solo, but I'd ditched my partner hours ago, frustrated by the rules and regulations—and the distrustful glances she kept throwing at me. It was a recurring routine that pissed me off more than I should've allowed.

I worked better alone.

Inside, the venue was nothing more than a rundown warehouse of patched concrete. Four levels rose above me like a maze, full of clubbers and Light knew what else. Music vibrated through the structure, feeding into my heightened senses. I'd always wanted time off to go clubbing at the city's premier alternative club, but there was never any rest for a Natural. This was as good as it was going to get.

Adrenaline was a place outsiders could come and express themselves without fear of being ridiculed, which was an admirable feat, but no one ever stopped to think about how the outsiders judged their own just as harshly. It was a human failing, despite striving for acceptance beyond the norm.

Then there was the other drawback of being different. Goths—more than any other human subculture—dabbled in demonic summoning the most. I didn't know why humans would want to mess with the Dark, but I knew there were humans out there who thrived on shock value. Wearing a corset as an outer layer, shaving half your hair off and colouring it black and blue, wasn't enough for some people.

Following the blip on my Light radar, I moved

through the club, rising through the heaving mass of bodies. I passed a room playing traditional goth music and narrowed my eyes at the humans twisting their hands towards the ceiling, their long, lace sleeves trailing through the mist from a smoke machine. It was a dance dubbed 'cobwebs in the ceiling'.

Snorting, I passed the door and kept climbing. It wasn't until I reached the top that I stopped. The stench of demonic activity was potent—the putrid fart smell curling my nose. It was no wonder no one else seemed to notice it. The club was a melting pot of scents—stale beer, sweat, urinal cakes, the sickly aroma from the smoke machine, and the damp that always clung to old buildings like this one. No amount of pine disinfectant could cover all of that.

The bass of a heavy industrial song reverberated through the concrete floor, pulsing up my legs and into my body. The flashing lights cast an eerie glow over the goths dancing around me, their movements stuttering like an elaborate stop-motion animation.

It wasn't hard to spot my target. It had leeched its Darkness all over the club like a putrid snail trail.

I watched the demon slide up against a woman in a sleek, black PVC corset. It'd inhabited a man's body or had taken on the appearance of one. I wouldn't know until I got closer.

It seemed the rarer cast of demons had fallen out of the woodwork since the rift had closed. The lesser, more rotting kind had fallen apart in the last few years and the big boys had come out to play in their frantic search for power. It meant demon hunting had become a wild new frontier.

They began to dance together, her hands snaking around his neck. *If only she knew.*

But I did, and it made watching its seduction even creeper knowing it was after her soul.

That's when I realised it'd screwed me over.

The club was a tight space, every inch used to its full capacity. That meant there were no dark corners or storage closets to drag my prey inside. I couldn't draw my arondight blade without hurting an innocent, and I couldn't do an exorcism because its putrid demonic arse would just fly off into someone else. And then I'd have to repeat the whole ordeal over again…and I loathed repeating myself.

It was a fight that might end badly, no matter what I did. I risked exposure of our kind by confronting it here, or the soul of an innocent if I choose to stand down.

I sighed. I couldn't walk away knowing I would damn her soul to complete erasure, despite her crimes to fashion.

The only way to end this was to wrestle the demon outside.

I slid through the crowd, silent and invisible, flowing past flailing arms and stomping boots, my form melting through the flashing lights. The demon didn't notice me until I was upon them.

I pressed my hand on the woman's shoulder, sending a flutter of Light—the magic that set me apart from humanity—into her. She blinked, then moved away from the threat, her gaze passing straight through the man she'd just been rubbing up against as if he'd never been there.

Once she was gone, I pulled the demon into the aura of my cloak, concealing it from the surrounding humans.

"Natural," it hissed.

"No soul eating for you tonight," I declared, closing my hand around its throat. "How about you and I take this outside?"

"Stupid girl. You're going to die."

It lunged, sending me flying back into the wall of dancers. The crowd parted, clubbers looking around to see what had pushed them out of the way.

I landed flat on my back with the creature on top of me, its hands clawing at my neck.

The moment skin touched skin, I could sense what it was. It wasn't an Infernal—a cloudy essence possessing a human—it was something else. Something new. It was evolving to survive in a world cut off from its power source. We'd been warned about this.

Its tongue grew, as did the barbs along it, and licked towards my face. I pushed my Light into it, my free hand scrambling for my arondight blade. The creature screeched as my power burned its flesh.

Our desperate struggle was cut short as the demon burst into a fireball above me. Gasping, I covered my face with my arm as heat blasted my exposed skin.

My Light went into overdrive. I pushed off the

floor, flipping to my feet. My hand closed around my sword hilt as I looked for my rescuer…or assailant—I wasn't quite sure what I'd just walked into.

An ebb of unknown power drew my attention to a man lingering in the shadows and our gazes met.

Tall, dark, and handsome had nothing on this guy. Sharp, angled jaw, piercing eyes, shaved head, lean muscle, dressed in black…but he wasn't a clubber. He wore jeans that were torn at the knees, battered combat boots, a tight, washed-out T-shirt, and a leather biker jacket that had seen better days. Rugged and dangerous—just how I liked my men, which made him a threat.

He lifted his finger to his lips, his eyes flashed silver as the strobe light pulsed above us.

I froze, my Light sensing the Darkness lingering just below the surface of his human exterior. It was also in that moment that I realised my cloak had failed and the entire fourth floor of *Adrenaline* was staring at me.

The man smirked and melted into the gap between a girl with a massive teased mohawk and a guy in black PVC pants and matching waist cincher.

I lunged after him, pushing through the humans. They shouted at me over the pounding music, but I wasn't focused on them. A flash of tired black leather led me out the door and down the stairs. Barrelling past a swarm of startled goths, I chased my newest target through the club, ducking under outstretched arms and twisting around stomping cyber goths on yet another dance floor.

A demon killing one of its own kind? Stranger things had happened, but they rarely went down like this. I got the feeling the newcomer was helping me out, but I'd learned from an early age not to have such high hopes in people, demonic or otherwise.

I could be running into another trap, but this was too strange not to follow up.

Just as security rushed into the venue, I made it outside where I was invisible again.

I legged it down the lane, my Light propelling me over the slick cobblestones, and veered around the corner. Following the whiff of Dark, I turned left in time to catch sight of my target ducking into another lane ahead.

Chasing him, I skidded around the building. Leaping into the air, I propelled myself over the row of parked motorcycled and mopeds, grazed a spiked fence, and landed in the terrace gardens. They were locked green spaces for the private use of the people living in the posh houses either side, but tonight they were just yet another obstacle in a chase scene.

I paid no attention to the night around me as I sprinted down the path, following the demon. Ahead, he jumped into a tree, then swung from a light pole.

Preempting his next move, I sprang over the fence and pushed off the ground with a burst of Light. I flew through the air and drew my arondight blade. Landing on the roof of the terrace, my boots clattered against the old terracotta tiles.

I was in the man's path.

I swung my sword, the blade erupting out of the

hilt. Silver shards of Light sparked as it slammed into the brick chimney stack centimetres from his face. He'd barely come to a halt in time, but luckily for him, we both had a second sight for these kinds of situations.

"I'd be careful with that thing," he said. "You could take someone's eye out."

They were the first words he had spoken, and his accent threw me. It was Scottish, but it wasn't. Another twang hid in there, though I couldn't figure it out.

"Give me one good reason why I shouldn't send you back to Hell," I demanded.

"Only one? I can give you a thousand." He smirked.

He began to move, and I forced my blade towards his face, but he ducked, avoiding the blow too fast for my liking. I pirouetted, arcing a full three-sixty degrees, only to slam my sword on the other side of the chimney stack, blocking his path again.

"Okay, okay," he said, holding up his hands as silver sparks danced across the roof.

"Start. *Talking.*"

"I've got no fight with you, Natural, but I can't be caught here."

I narrowed my eyes, my gaze piercing his Darkness. That's when I saw it—something I recognised from a long time ago. I knew what to look for, because I'd had the same thing growing inside me —a mutation. "You're not entirely Dark."

He smirked. "Takes one to know one."

I hesitated, and that split-second gave him an opening to strike.

He pushed me backwards with a pulse of Darkness and wrenched my blade from my hand. My boot slipped on the tiled roof and I was falling.

Air rushed past me and I let go of my Light, the burst of energy softening the blow as I landed flat on my back in the garden. My sword speared the ground next to my head, the blade imbedding so close, I felt the breeze flutter against my cheek. My heart leapt into my throat and I pushed to my feet, cursing.

Son of a…

I wrenched my arondight blade free and took off after the man. I was not letting him get away.

Human Convergence was dead. It'd ended forever the night the rift had closed. Scarlett and Wilder—the Twin Flames—had killed Mordred, the source of all demonic mutations, and we'd been cured. *We'd been cured.*

I jumped off the end of the row of terrace houses and landed on the footpath of Islington High Street. I stood on the corner, watching as a red double-decker bus zoomed past, and threw my hands into the air.

The man was gone.

2

———

The Light and the Dark. Capitals and all.

The Light was the power wielded by the Naturals, handed down by the celestial being known to us as the Lady of the Lake. Who she was or where she'd gone to, was unknown.

The Dark was the essence that made up all demonic life. Where it came from was a mystery. The only truths known were that the Dark had swept over countless parallel universes, consuming and destroying all life in its path. When Camelot was torn apart by the celestial power held within the swords Arondight and Excalibur, they had unknowingly opened the way to let them through.

Since Arondight and Excalibur had been reborn into two Natural warriors—Scarlett and Wilder—the balance had tipped in the Light's favour. They'd closed the rift, defeated the One—the leader of all demon-kind—and the world was now recovering from eight hundred years of war.

Still, the reality of who we were and what we still faced was hidden from humanity, as it always had been, which was why I was now standing in front of the leader of the Naturals.

The Inquisitor. Wilder Pendragon, aka Excalibur himself.

I felt my cheeks heat as he glared at me. So, it wasn't the friendly reunion I'd been hoping for, but at least I got to see him, right?

Famous last words.

"I read your report," he said, his voice echoing through the empty assembly chamber.

"Yes, uh…" I didn't know what to call him anymore. Wilder, Mr. Pendragon, Excalibur…sir.

"Abandoning your partner, following a demon into a crowded area, confronting it." He sighed and pinched the bridge of his nose. He looked tired, and it might've been the fact that he was the Argent Flame —silver by nature—but he had more grey hairs than the last time I saw him. All the bureaucracy must weigh him down. "And you lost your cloak."

"It must have been when the demon burned," I said. "I uh… I didn't notice I was uncloaked before that."

The Inquisitor grunted, unimpressed. "You didn't notice?"

I shook my head. Sheepish had nothing on how I felt.

"Fortunately for you, no one saw anything," he went on. "All those humans saw was a woman sprawled on the floor."

"How do you know?"

"Romy and Alo were in the vicinity. They arrived at the scene not long after you left and cleaned up your mess."

I didn't know what was worse—being torn to shreds by the Inquisitor or disappointing your hero's best friends. Scarlett was going to find out what I'd done eventually and…and nothing.

I hadn't seen or spoken to Scarlett Ravenwood—aka Arondight—for almost a year. She was off being all important and didn't have any time for me anymore. Even my parents were out of communication range.

Wilder's brow furrowed. "What's going on with you, Madeleine?"

I asked myself the same question daily.

After I'd graduated and became a Natural warrior, things were great…for a while. Soon it became clear my past was going to be a hurdle too high for some people to overcome.

While a senior at the Academy, an Infernal infected by Human Convergence had possessed me—the Dark's attempt at creating an army out of humanity—and mutated me to the point I'd almost lost my Light. It'd all been a plot to bring down a horde of demons on the Academy to destroy the entire next generation of Natural warriors.

Scarlett and everyone told me the attack wasn't my fault, but how could I believe them? I'd been stupid enough to get myself compromised. I'd opened the metaphoric door and let them in. If it wasn't for me, the wards would've held and…

Despite being cured, people still looked at me like I was stuffed with twisted Darkness—and for once, it had nothing to do with my fashion choices.

"Madeline?"

I rolled my eyes. "Oh yeah, there was that time I was almost mutated into a demon as a teenager. That might have something to do with it."

"Prejudice is a trait of our past, not our future."

"And you can't turn it off with a flick of a switch. People thought you were a demon, but you turned out to be Excalibur. I was just a demon. No one's forgotten."

"I've been where you are," he told me. "I almost lost everything rebelling against it, just like you are now."

"Until Scarlett," I said, my heart twisting. "Not everyone has a Scarlett or a Wilder."

"This isn't about us. It's about your dangerous need to risk your life regardless of others and the exposure of our kind. You've seen more than anyone your age and experience. I hoped that you'd understand the need for upholding the tenants of the Codex the most out of anyone. I expected better from you, Madeline."

I closed off my expression and became a wall of stone. It was tough when your boss' boss' boss—who once helped save me from full demonic mutation—still saw me as a kid.

"Get on with it then," I drawled.

Wilder thumped his fist down on the table. "You're being reassigned," he barked. "The London Sanctum does not require the services of a rogue Natural."

"What?" I argued. "But London is—"

"I have already made the decision."

I lowered my gaze, knowing that disputing Wilder's orders would only make things worse. "W-Where am I going?"

He scraped his chair back and rose to his feet. "Camelot."

Mist clung to the hills, settling into the dips in the valley. The sun was out, but it didn't stop the chill that was settling into my bones.

I grasped the roll bar on the pickup truck as it bounced over the rough track. My arse balanced precariously on the edge of the tray, but it was the only seat available.

I was the only grunt amongst the party. The others who sat in the back with me—two men and three women—were all researchers, archeologists, and scientists. Little flags stitched on their black duffle bags told me they were from all over the world—Canada, USA, Australia, South Africa. Unearthing Camelot had become an international Natural affair.

The human world knew this place as the Clee Hills. The area was known for its rolling green landscape and ruined Medieval past. Some of the highest peaks were located here—if eighteen hundred feet of grass-covered rock could be considered a mountain.

Ruined castles and villages dotted here and there, and ancient quarries still carved holes in the bedrock beneath. It was an archaeologist's dream, but it was nothing compared to what hid beyond the veil cast by the Naturals.

The others were craning their necks, searching for the first glimpse of the castle, but my mind was elsewhere. I wouldn't call it sulking, but I wasn't necessarily jumping for joy, either.

I bristled thinking about the report that'd landed me in front of the Inquisitor. It was bad enough that I'd been reassigned, but when Wilder found out about the mystery man…? Being given a new babysitting gig would be the least of my worries.

It wasn't until later that I realised the man shouldn't have been able to keep my arondight blade active, not unless he was made of Light.

I don't know why I left him out of my report. The existence of a demon-hybrid was bad news, but… I didn't have the words to finish my reasoning.

The pickup came to a stop and the Naturals began to pile out the back. I swung my legs over the edge and pushed off, landing with a thud on the hard ground. While I'd been brooding, we'd passed through the ancient wards concealing the dig site.

I shouldered my duffle bag and lingered with the others as they gaped up at the outer edges of the castle. When I thought of Camelot, I'd pictured a castle with a few turrets, a gate, and maybe a moat—like Disneyland, but with more holes. Now that I was standing here, I realised the real thing was far larger than I'd ever expected.

Camelot wasn't a castle, it was a city.

No wonder they'd only uncovered less than five percent of the site. I'd rolled my eyes and presumed they were just being slow, but the massive structure I was staring up at was only the outer wall. We hadn't even glimpsed the destruction that'd torn the inner castle apart.

The wall rose like a silent monolith through the fog, made of solid granite nearly seventy feet tall. One end seemed to carve straight into the cliff face—the natural formation used to its full advantage. The other had crumbled around what used to be an outer postern gate, and stone blocks the size of the pickup were strewn across the hillside. Grass and heath had grown up around them in the last few hundred years, so they now seemed to be part of the modern landscape.

"Madeleine!"

I looked up to see Aiden Thompson walk down to meet us. His Wellington boots were caked in mud and the sticky clay made him stumble down the track like he had two left feet. It was hard to pair the reality to the surface of the man on first glance. I wanted to say he was a handsome Italian Indiana Jones-type archeologist with superpowers, but he was just a massive nerd with a mini-pickaxe.

It was easy to see why all the researchers fawned

over him, but I couldn't understand it. He was awkward, his clothes were always rumpled, and his curly brown hair was a bird's nest. Despite his indifference to his appearance—which a little manscaping would fix—he was intelligent, passionate, and dedicated to unearthing the secrets lost in the cataclysm.

I looked up to Aiden like a student did to a teacher. Fitting, considering he used to be my history professor at the Academy. There was only ten years difference in age between us, but it felt like a chasm after that relationship.

Then there was that time I tried to frame him as a demon-hybrid. Oh, and that other bit where I'd tried kill him.

He stood before me and drew me in for a hug, much to the chagrin of the new batch of female researchers. I tensed and clapped him on the back, hoping it was enough to satisfy. I didn't like to hug.

"When Wilder said he transferred you, I didn't believe him," Aiden said, pulling away. He looked amused and I wasn't sure if it was over the awkward hug, or the fact that I was standing in the mud at Camelot. "But here you are!"

"Yep." I popped the p at the end and glanced at the others. I considered this posting a punishment while they thought it was the biggest break of their lives. Already, I could see the exasperated loathing on their faces when they looked at me.

"Yes. Well." Aiden coughed. "Hi all." He waved at the newcomers like he was wiping condensation off a window. "I'm Aiden Thompson, the head of the archaeological team here at Camelot. I suck at speeches, so let's get you all inside. We've set up base camp inside the wall." He gestured the group forwards. "Welcome to Camelot."

I let the group filter past, ignoring the jealous glares from the women. I wondered if Aiden realised just how hot half the female population of the site was for him. Knowing him, probably not.

Sighing, I gave one last look at the world outside Camelot. Then I turned and followed my fate up the hill. My boots squelched in churned mud as I dawdled behind the group.

"Camelot exists on the fringes of our reality," Aiden said. "Time and space are folded here, which means the inside is much larger than the outside."

"To think we used to have so much power and understanding," one woman said. Miss Canada. She was a scientist. "It's unbelievable."

"I wonder how they managed it," one man added.

"The Druids," I said with a huff. Everyone turned to stare at me, and I swallowed my annoyance. "They could walk between universes and change time."

"That's one theory," Aiden said cheerfully. "Many of the artefacts we've unearthed point to Merlin having a hand in the construction. Not so much the outer city, but the castle itself."

We moved through to another area of the outer ring of the complex.

"As you know, Camelot was torn apart in the cataclysm," Aiden went on, firmly wedged in his happy place, "and the Dark took hold of it, making it its base. Reality was twisted, and the creatures that lived here were at their most powerful. That was due to their close proximity to their own world."

"What happened to them?" one of the men asked.

"The demons who lived here?" Aiden shrugged. "When the rift was sealed and the One was defeated, their hold on Camelot was severed. Without any power to feed from, they fled. They're likely wasting away, hidden out in the world someplace."

"Preying on innocents," the Australian researcher said.

"Thank goodness for the Sanctums," Miss Canada remarked.

I snorted as we passed another broken wall and stepped into a clearing the size of a soccer pitch. This was where base camp had been erected. A small tent city stretched before me, bustling with activity.

Portable generators were rumbling happily, powering everything from research tents and medical, to the kitchen, showers, and dormitories. Naturals bustled from tent to tent, and in the distance, I could see movement within the lower city of Camelot.

Aiden gathered everyone close. "It's been a long day of travel for all of you, so we'll begin your new assignments tomorrow. For now, get some rest and settle in. The real work starts at sunrise."

The researchers began to mutter excitedly amongst themselves, wandering off through the tent city, their heads swivelling in all directions as they went.

I stood on the edge of the camp, wondering where the grunts went. There had to be a designated place for the security detail.

"Madeleine," Aiden said, gesturing to me.

I turned, my duffle almost colliding with a passing Natural, who almost dropped the box they were carrying. My cheeks heated and I began to realised just how out of place I was here.

"Wilder mentioned—"

"I know what he mentioned," I interrupted.

"And what's that?"

My jaw tensed. "Demon is as demon does."

"You're still hung up on that?" he asked, his shoulders slumping. "Madeline."

"People keep telling me it was the demon inside me that did those things, but it only possessed me for a moment. All those things were me. *I* did them. You can't tell me you don't see how people look at me."

"A mutation made you do those things. You had no control over them."

"I tried to kill you."

"You weren't yourself."

I narrowed my eyes. "So, what am I supposed to be doing here?"

"Security," Aiden said with a sigh. "Escort detail. Patrol."

So nothing even remotely interesting.

"Madeleine…if you open yourself up, you could find things aren't as drastic as you make them out to be."

I'd never fit in before I'd been possessed, but

afterwards it was even clearer there was no place for me—and that was what I struggled with the most. I'd always carry the stigma of being demon bound and not a damn thing I could do would change it.

"Don't worry about pointing me to the command tent," I said, moving past him. "I'm more than capable of finding it myself."

3

———

I swept open the flap on the command tent.

Caleb Thompson stood hunched over a table, swiping his finger back and forth across a tablet. Aiden's older brother was the warrior of the family. They both had similar colouring—dark and broody— but the elder seemed to have all the coordination the younger lacked.

He wore standard issue black tactical gear, his jacket open and his arondight blade strapped to his waist. The hilt flashed silver in the murky light

Sensing my arrival, he looked up. "Madeleine. I was wondering when you were arriving."

"Sir." I let the flap fall back into place, closing out the hubbub of the camp.

The tent was draughty, but there was a Light-generated heater in the centre which fended off most of the chill. Someone had pinned various maps to boards and tables, and there was a glaring lack of weaponry. Who needed a rack of cold iron blades guarding a ruin? Not us.

A row of black storage boxes were stacked to one side, the stamps on the side marking them as drones. I assumed they were for surveying the ruins more than surveillance. We'd never needed technology to do our jobs—that's what our Light was for.

"I'm glad to have someone of your capabilities here, Madeline, but I want to make something clear. There is no place for theatrics, lone wolves, or self-serving ambition at Camelot. We uphold the tenants of our people here, just as any other outpost."

I held his gaze. He'd read my file.

"I don't care what the Inquisitor says, this isn't a low-priority mission," he went on, throwing in a little dig towards Wilder—there was no love lost there. "The work being done here at Camelot is important and it needs to be protected. There is no telling what might be unearthed here—demonic or otherwise."

I supposed there was truth in that, but it wasn't the front lines. Maybe I was crazy, but that's where I wanted to be. All my life I'd dreamed about serving the London Sanctum and fighting the Dark—that's where the centre of all Natural-kind was and it housed the Codex.

The Codex was the book that housed our sacred history. Created in the cataclysm's aftermath, it was intended to save as much of our lost heritage as possible, but over the years, it'd become much more than a record. It governed our choices, our beliefs, and our very souls. The manuscript had gathered so much Light it had become a link to all Naturals…but only one could read it. The Protector—and the Twin Flames.

Then there was the bit where anyone who touched it burned to ash from the inside out. We were a delightful bunch of supernaturals.

The point was, everyone wanted a post in London. *Everyone*. But since I was standing here of all places, I'd obviously screwed it up.

Thompson stared at me, his gaze cold and heavy. "Are we on the same page?"

I read everything I needed to from his expression. He wasn't a man I should push too hard.

"Sir."

His eyes narrowed slightly and sighed. "Report in the morning. I'll have your schedule fixed by then." He nodded towards the tent flap. "The barracks are at the outer edges of camp. They've been marked."

I picked up my duffle. "Sir."

"Madeline?"

I lingered, waiting for his parting wisdom.

"You can say more to me than *sir*."

"Yes…sir."

He snorted and shoved his hand through his hair. "That's a start, I suppose." He moved around the table and stood before me. Thompson was a full head taller and I had to lift my chin to meet his gaze. "Just so we're on the same page, this is your last chance, Madeline. I'm not sure what will happen to you if you screw this up."

I tensed. This was a new revelation. Wilder was

testing me by not mentioning my precarious position and Thompson was throwing me a bone.

"You're an exceptional Natural," he went on, "that much is clear from your file. Top grades at the Academy, high strike rates…but your attitude is severely lacking. The red flags almost outweigh the accolades. You're far too young and talented to be discharged for insubordination."

I bit my tongue as shame pulsed through my body. Rebelliousness would only get me so far, then it was a sharp turn to a cliff called 'fall from grace'. He was right—everyone who tried to beat it into my head was —but I didn't know how to be anything other than a pain in the arse.

Thompson relaxed his posture. "The only person who can help you is yourself. We can only do so much."

"I know, sir. I… I'm trying to figure it out."

He sighed again. "I sincerely hope so." He nodded towards the flap. "Now get out of my sight."

After I'd found an empty bunk, I followed my nose to the camp kitchen.

The sun was already lowering in the sky and many of the Naturals working up on the dig site were returning to base for the evening.

I sat at a table in the corner—away from the noise —and watched as they filed into the tent. It was easy to tell everyone apart from the amount of dirt caked on their clothes. Hard mud on both knees equalled archaeologist. Caked boots and weaponry were security. Mostly clean were scientists who spent most of their time in their laboratories. Spotless were the researchers who catalogued and translated.

I poked at my food, the battered fork spearing the soggy vegetables.

There seemed to be at least seventy to eighty people here. Not a great deal when Camelot inhabited a twenty square kilometre pocket of space and time. And Aiden mentioned they'd uncovered less than five percent of that.

"You're pouting. I can see nothing's changed."

I jumped as a familiar face appeared in my line of vision and dropped my fork. "Trent?"

He grinned and sat across from me. "The one and only."

Trent had grown up a lot since I'd last seen him. His face seemed to have learned what stubble was and the boyish roundness in his cheeks had hardened. The hair on his head had darkened and his eyes seemed more focused than I remembered.

"Look at you," I said, trying to remember the last time I'd seen him. "You've gone and grown up."

"Physically," he said with a grin. "Mentally?" He pulled a face. "The jury's still out on that one."

"How's Kayla?" I quipped, raising an eyebrow. Kayla was the Natural who he'd had the hots for throughout our time at the Academy. Along with being the most popular girl in the place, she was also the school bully who'd made my life a living hell. I'd tried to kill her when I was a mutant demon, which was an annoying recurring theme.

"Get with the times, Mads," he proclaimed. "Kayla and I broke up a year ago."

I tilted my head to the side. "Still a sore point?"

"It didn't work long-term. Shite happens. But I wanna know where you've been. You never write or call."

"People drift apart after school," I told him.

"Humans say those kinds of things. We're different. War can't tear us apart, Mads."

I shrugged. "Sorry. I've never been good with people skills. I don't think my life is that interesting."

"*Mads*. We were born to be interesting."

I pointed my fork at him, secretly glad he was here. After everything that'd happened at the Academy, the senior class and I had all become fast friends, but lost touch after graduation. "You know I don't like it when you call me Mads."

Another tray clattered down next to mine and I looked up to find another familiar face from my tumultuous school days.

"Crikey," Maisy declared, sitting down, "if it isn't Madeleine Greenbriar, come to grace us with her presence."

"What kind of word is crikey?" I asked, screwing up my face.

"I learned it from the Australians," she replied. "It's occa for OMG."

Trent snorted and leaned back in his chair. "Does

it comfort you knowing some things never change, Mads?"

Maisy had always been on the outer edges of the mean girl trio that ruled the Academy. Kayla was the queen and Maisy and Trisha had been her little worker bees. She'd been part of the bullying, but apologised and make amends after the attack. We'd come together when it'd mattered the most, so I supposed it was progress.

I narrowed my eyes at Trent. Talking about personal growth—his smart mouth hadn't progressed with the stubble on his chin. "What's Kayla doing now?"

"We don't talk about her," Maisy whispered.

"She knows about the breakup," Trent said, raising his voice. "No need to whisper. I'm over her."

Maisy snorted and rolled her eyes, signalling she thought he wasn't. Trent always talked a big game.

I didn't care to know all the sordid details, so I turned the conversation around. "What about Trisha, then?"

"She finally got her posting in New York," Maisy said.

"She went to America?" I asked. "Why?"

"After her sister, Alicia, was killed in the Dark Night attacks, she wanted to see where she'd made her life," Maisy explained. "Alicia was head of some special task force. Pretty covert work, apparently."

The Dark Night. It had a dramatic flair to it, but it fit the devastation those few hours, five years ago, had caused. In the weeks before the rift had closed, the demon-hybrid Mordred had led a coordinated attack on Sanctums all over the world. In the aftermath—after we'd won the war—the truth of the devastation had finally been revealed and it was worse than we'd known. New York, Los Angeles, Sydney, Rome, Paris, Cape Town, Lima, Tokyo, and London had fallen. It was the worst loss the Naturals had faced since the cataclysm. Still, the balance had tipped so far into the Light that the Dark barely had any holes left to hide in.

"Ever heard of the mole people?" Trent asked.

I frowned. "Mole people?"

He nodded. "There's an urban legend amongst the humans about people who live in the underground transit network underneath Manhattan—the subway as they call it there. Demons congregate in piss and shite, but the New York Sanctum believed there was more to the mole people than just myth."

"They were mapping the tunnels hidden by Darkness when the Sanctum fell," Maisy said. "They thought something was buried underneath the city, but never got the chance to find out."

"Isn't this supposed to be covert?" I asked.

"Not anymore. Word got out in the chaos. It's public knowledge these days."

"So…" Trent leaned his elbows on the table and gave me a fierce look, "why are you here? London get boring or something?"

I lowered my gaze. "I, uh—"

"She got into trouble again," Maisy told him.

"How do you know?" I demanded.

She laughed and shook her head. "She's forgotten how the rumour mill works."

I glanced over my shoulder at the surrounding tables. A few heads turned away and a few more wore glares designed especially for me.

"I haven't forgotten," I murmured. "I'm not afforded that luxury."

Trent frowned and followed my gaze.

"They don't like me being here," I told him.

"Screw them," he declared. "They don't know you, Madeleine. We do, and it's their loss."

I sighed and speared a potato with my fork. It was far too soggy to be considered roasted and split down the middle.

"You get that reaction a lot, don't you?" Maisy asked.

"Let's just say, I understand how Wilder felt all those years ago."

"He was able to overcome it," Trent told me.

Maisy kicked him underneath the table. "Yeah, by becoming Excalibur."

"Great." I rolled my eyes. "All I have to do is save the world from eternal war and I'll be elevated to normal status. Good to know."

"Don't worry about them, Madeleine," Maisy said. "Just follow your training and no one can hold anything against you."

Easier said than done.

"Are both of you on security?" I asked.

"Yeah," Maisy replied. "I don't know what people have told you, but it's not so bad."

That surprised me. "I thought it would be dead up here. Pardon the pun."

"Now and then we get a lone demon who will lurk around the wall," Trent told me. "It was their home away from home for a few centuries, so they live in hope, I guess."

"Animal instinct," Maisy said.

"All the lesser demons are dead," I reminded her. "You don't think the ones who are left aren't at least a little intelligent?"

"Define intelligent," Trent replied with a smirk. "Camelot is crawling with Naturals, yet they still try."

"Desperate hope," Maisy said, looking out the clear side of the tent. The tip of the tallest tower of Camelot's inner bailey was just visible in the fading sunlight.

"Maybe they left something behind," Trent mused.

The undiscovered dangers of Camelot. It reminded me of a trashed council flat after the tenants had moved out and left their rubbish behind. There was no telling what the Dark had discarded in the city. Perhaps it was a dirtier job than I'd first realised.

"You can hardly blame them for trying to get back in," Maisy added. "I know I would."

Sympathising with a demon. I guess that was one thing that made us different from the Dark—our ability to empathise.

"Yeah," I said, ignoring the simmering hostility around me, "maybe you're right."

4

———

The night was clear. Stars shone across the sky and the moon illuminated the rolling hills with an eerie silver hue.

I stood on a hill to the northeast of Camelot, the darkness wrapping around me like a blanket. I'd always preferred dark places—they seemed private in such a busy world. Open spaces unsettled me, as if the breadth of the sky would swallow me whole.

Patrolling wasn't so bad. Missions were rigorous and structured, whereas walking the streets was more fluid. Anything could happen. Out here though, it was lonely and drab. I wasn't sure I was cut out for the country lifestyle.

I'd been paired with Trent, which was both a blessing and a curse. The blessing was that he was familiar. The curse was that he wouldn't let me get the slip on him. It'd been five years since we'd graduated, but he remembered all my tricks.

Still, I had to make this work.

Our path had taken us farther away from Camelot than I imagined it would have. There wasn't much chance of a wayward hiker stumbling across the ruined castle—the wards and cloaking took care of that—but Thompson wanted us to head off any demon who came prowling. It was a sound plan considering most of the personnel on the dig weren't trained warriors.

I looked out over the valley, the lights of the camp hidden behind the crumbling walls. Blinking, I was able to tune out my awareness of the energy hiding the city—one minute it was there, the next it was gone.

"You should see it in the day time," Trent said, standing next to me. "From this angle, you can almost see the chasm in the centre of the castle."

"Has anyone been there?"

"Just an exploratory team a few years ago. No one else has been down there since Scarlett and Wilder sealed the rift."

I grunted and cast my gaze elsewhere. It was quiet. I was used to the constant noise and movement of London, so the absence of everything but nature was a little jarring.

"You're so angry at the world," Trent said. "Isn't it exhausting?"

"You'd think blind hatred is exhausting, but it seems to be a bottomless well of rechargeable energy. If only humans could use it to run their dirty power plants, then they wouldn't debate the existence of global warming and rising sea levels."

"You're so intense," he stated. "You exhaust me sometimes."

"No," I said, continuing along the trail, "it's not exhausting. It's all I've known."

He followed me, his boots crunching on loose stone. "That's a lie. After the attack on the Academy—"

I spun around. "A fleeting glimpse of something better is not enough to change someone's life."

Trent shook his head, the moonlight glinting off the arondight blade at his waist. "I'm not going to convince you, am I?"

I knew what I had to do—I had to make peace with the things I'd done in my past, no matter who was to blame for them—I just wasn't sure how to get there.

"No one can hold my hand through this," I told him. "I have to find my own way."

He didn't reply. Instead, we looked out over the valley towards the lights of the human village of Ludlow. They shimmered in the distance, unaware of what was hidden mere miles from their cozy cottages.

"What's it like at the London Sanctum?" Trent asked.

"Frustrating."

"I don't believe you. Being stationed in London wouldn't be anything close to that."

I'd loved to tell him it'd lived up to all my expectations, but things had changed in recent years. If anyone had bothered to ask me, I would have told them that I thought we relied too much on Arondight and Excalibur. That we were making the same mistakes Arthur and Lancelot had. That we'd dropped our guard when we should've kept it up.

The reemergence of a mutated demon-hybrid was proof of that, but for some bizarre reason, I kept that nugget of information to myself.

I blinked, an image of the man flashing in my mind's eye. His form melting into the shadows at *Adrenaline*, the strobe lights masking his appearance. The silver flash of his eyes as I stood before him on that rooftop.

"Madeleine?"

I bit my lip and cleared my head. "Don't you feel like we've become complacent?"

"No. We can relax a little after centuries of fighting. How is that complacent?"

"The rift is closed but demons still lurk in the world."

"Yeah, everyone knows that."

"There's always one last gasp." I didn't think he understood what I was getting at. The last gasp was when violence grew as the enemy desperately tried to hang onto any scrap of power it could. "Now is not the time to drop our guard."

He rolled his eyes. "Take a beat, Madeline."

"They're evolving, Trent," I snapped. "You don't think that poses a threat?"

He blew a frustrated breath through his lips. "You're so intense."

"And you're too..." I waved my hands at him,

trying to think of a word, *"mellow*. Babysitting history nerds has made you sloppy."

"And your arrogance has blinded you to the fact that someone has been watching us for the past five minutes, so who's the moron now?"

I froze, my anger melting away. "Why didn't you say so?"

"You should've known so."

Five shadows oozed from behind the rocks and slunk across the hillside, moving quickly. They bore down on our position and we were forced to draw our arondight blades. Time to stand our ground.

As they approached, I realised they weren't just any demons. At least not the ones I'd been expecting.

They weren't Infernals possessing the bodies of humans, or the rotting carcasses of lesser creatures. They were actual demons—creatures that'd crawled their way out of the rift over eight hundred years ago, powerful enough to haul their bodies with them.

Their long arms and legs were tipped with clawed hands and feet that shimmered with Darkness. They'd evolved to appear humanoid, though their size had diminished since their arrival on Earth. Cut off from their master—the One—their power had waned, but they'd learned how to adapt.

I was entirely sure these things would be able to walk through a shopping mall in broad daylight and look just like everyone else, but to our Natural eyes, they were revealed for what they truly were. *Monsters.*

"Did you say something about evolving?" Trent asked, his hand closing around his arondight blade.

"I'm not so sure about that," I replied. "They look like they're the scum-sucking evictees of Camelot."

"Well?" Trent asked the demons. "Are you?"

"Somehow, I don't think they're into chatting," I drawled.

At the sound of my voice, all five heads turned towards me. *Freaky*.

Trent eyed me, flashing me a subtle signal. I spun my arondight blade hand over hand and together, we struck.

My sword collided with razor-sharp claws, sending sparks of Light across the hillside. Metal dragged along the length before sliding clear. I'd barely finished my stroke before I was forced to twist and block a blow at my back.

I pirouetted, sent a blast of Light to the side, then kicked at the demon lunging at my front. I was vaguely aware of Trent's sword sparking as he clashed with a demon father down the trail. Somehow, we'd become separated, the demons worming their way between us until our strength was split in half. *Shite on it*.

It wasn't an easy fight. The demons I'd fought in the city were slow and sluggish or were Infernals who could be pried from the bodies of their hosts. These creatures were stronger, faster, and Darkness seeped into their bones. Their blows struck hard, jarring up my arms, and I barely had enough Light to dodge their menacing claws.

I cried out as I was backhanded, my head snapping to the side. I slipped on the loose gravel of the trail, almost pitching over the edge and down the ravine.

Anchoring my heel, I arced my blade towards the closest demon. It wailed as the metal imbedded in its side, the gash spewing black blood and white-hot sparks. The creature's head lolled back, opening its grotesque mouth, then lowered its dark gaze to mine.

I tried to wrench my sword free, but it was stuck in the demon's side. It cackled, wrapping its hands around the blade as two more looked on in devilish amusement as their brother tore itself free and pushed the sword—and me—backwards.

My foot slipped, then I was falling.

Trent's panicked cry echoed somewhere above me. "*Madeline!*"

I rolled down the side of the hill, powerless to stop. My Light was just out of reach, my fear blocking the path. I'd have to wait until I hit the bottom—wherever that was. Rocks pummelled my body, the sting of cuts blooming everywhere.

The night spun around me as I attempted to control my momentum, but by this stage, I was in total free fall.

As the ground levelled out, I began to slow before I tumbled to a complete stop at the base of the hill. The impact had pushed all the air from my lungs, and I gasped, my chest burning.

I reached for my Light and a pulse ebbed through my body, dulling the pain. Standing, I realised I wasn't alone. Three demons had followed my chaotic fall and began to circle my position, surrounding me.

"She knows it," one rasped through its thin lips.

I turned as the demon behind me spoke. "We will take it."

My grip tightened around my arondight blade. "Take what?"

The third demon lifted its heavy arm and sent a pulse of Darkness towards me. There was nothing I could do to stop the wave from hitting me, and when it did, everything changed.

The unfamiliar spark I'd felt when I landed, flared. It wasn't the soothing smoothness of Light I was used to. It had a sharp tang that left my skin feeling electrified.

When I'd been mutated by Human Convergence, I'd always blacked out when the Dark side of my condition came out. Apart from a few fleeting flashes, I never remembered what I'd been doing. If my Light had turned Dark, I had no idea what it looked or felt like.

Whatever this spark was, it wasn't anything I'd encountered before. It was dark, intoxicating…*demonic*.

Let's just say I was starting to get why humans dabbled with dark magic. The addiction levels were high.

I stumbled and my boot caught on the loose rock underfoot. I fell, landing on my arse. My arondight blade slipped from my fingers and clattered across the rocky ground, the blade disappearing into the hilt. I lunged after it, barely avoiding the claws aimed at my chest, and cursed as it fell into a crack in the rock.

Sensing trouble behind me, I rolled as a large bolder slammed to the ground, splintering where my head had been a second ago.

I flipped to my feet, using the momentum to draw my cold iron dagger. I backed away, brandishing the blade as three demons advanced on my position.

Black eyes stared at me as claws dragged across the trail. My heart hammered in my chest as my mind raced over my options. Trent had his hands full up on the ridge, so I was on my own.

Bile rose in the back of my throat, but I wasn't sure if it was the 'imminent death' thing or the 'I might still be a demon' thing.

All three demons lunged at the same time and I swiped my dagger, cold iron colliding with flesh. It wasn't enough. Without my sword, I had no way of vanquishing their putrid arses. All I could do was hold my ground and pray to the Light.

I was shoved into a pair of slimy black arms. Pushing a pulse of Light into the demon, it screeched and let me go. I stabbed my dagger backwards, ramming it into the side of one of the others.

Damn, it was hard to tell these things apart—they all looked exactly the same.

I ducked under a swinging set of claws and gasped as I was struck in the lower back. The blow to my spine sent me reeling and I collapsed, losing my grip on the dagger.

A demon kicked me on the shoulder, and I was down for the count.

Staring up at the creatures, I began to regret a lot

of things. Being an arsehole to pretty much everyone. Not following orders. Being an arrogant bitch. Thinking I was better than everyone else. Believing I was invincible. Basically, I was a big fat disappointment to two thousand years of Natural history.

Clawed arms held me down and I thrashed as the third demon looked at me. Its slimy black skin shimmered in the moonlight, and when it opened its mouth, the stench of sulphur made me gag.

"We will take it," it hissed as its claws wrapped around my head. *It is ours.*

The last thing I saw before I lost consciousness was the creature's grotesque face as it lowered towards mine.

5

———

I woke some time later.

It was difficult to tell how long I'd been unconscious, but I found myself in almost complete darkness. I was lying on a damp rocky floor and the air was heavy with moisture. I shivered as cold seeped into my limbs.

Pushing to my elbows, I grimaced as my head throbbed. I reached for my Light…but it wasn't there. I searched within myself and came back empty-handed.

No, no, no…

Where the hell was I? Wherever those demons had taken me, they had a way to cut me off from my power. *This was bad.*

As my eyes adjusted, I began to make out shapes in the shimmer of torchlight that filtered in from somewhere beyond. The first thing I noticed were the bars. I fumbled in the low light, my hands scrambling over another bar and another, before scraping against stone. I went back the other direction with the same results.

I was in a cage deep underground. The thing about dark places buried underneath millions of tones of dirt? No one could hear you scream. Trust demons to lurk in a shite heap like this.

I curled my hands around the bars and shook them. The metal rattled but didn't budge.

Sinking back onto my arse, I grimaced when my side began to ache, joining my temples. I was beginning to understand just how much I'd been taking my Light for granted.

Small, loose stones littered the floor, and water trickled down fissures in the wall. The drip as droplets hit rocks echoed through the blackness. It was cold and the smell of damp and rot filled my nose.

I moved my gaze past the bars and gasped as I spotted an outline of a human form lurking in the shadows. Not sensing any Darkness, I scooted towards the bars and leaned against the rusty metal.

"Hey," I hissed, realising a man was propped up against the wall. "*Hey*. Trent, is that you?"

He didn't move. Reaching out, my fingers brushed against his arm and I recoiled. He was clammy to the touch and rigid…like a corpse. Beyond him, the shape of more bodies emerged from the gloom.

I gagged and huddled against the far corner of the cage. They were dead—just empty husks waiting for hosts.

It was a stockpile of faces hanging in a morbid

wardrobe. So, what did that make me? A pet guinea pig?

It could only mean one thing…a greater demon lurked somewhere close. My situation had gone from bad to worse in t-minus one second.

Gathering my courage, I crawled back to the bars and prodded at the corpse. His head lolled to the side and I managed to make out his features. It wasn't Trent. I couldn't be certain about the others, but greater demons didn't possess bodies that already had souls. Not usually.

A small shred of hope began to surface. If Trent wasn't among them, maybe he'd escaped and warned the others at Camelot.

I settled back against the wall and rubbed my side. My ribs didn't seem to be broken, but they sure felt like it. My head felt cracked and my temples throbbed, but there was nothing I could do to soothe the ache. My Light was dampened and whatever Darkness had flared inside me was gone.

Darkness.

We were all cured when Scarlett and Wilder had killed Mordred—the mutated Natural Human Convergence was synthesised from. My Light had returned and the Dark… A piece of demon mutation must lie dormant inside me. It was the only explanation and knowing I wasn't entirely Natural made me want to hurl.

Movement made my heart leap and I pressed back into the corner as the bars scraped back. Two inky black demons slunk into my prison and bore down on me.

I kicked out to fend them off, but they just cackled in amusement as they grabbed my arms and dragged me across the gravel floor.

Once I was clear of the cage, I searched for my Light, but it was still out of reach. What the hell had they done to me? I thrashed, but all I managed to do was tire myself out.

By the time they hauled me into a cavern deeper in the cave system, I'd figured out resistance was futile. Without my Light, I was as feeble as a human, and my injuries stung like hell.

Finally, they threw me onto the ground, my cheek slamming against cold limestone.

My eyes widened as I realised who my appointment was with. A sigil had been carved into the floor in front of me and the indentations rippled with blood. I knew whatever was going to happen wasn't going to be pretty. My fingers scraped against the rock as I tried to calm myself.

I'd been trained for every conceivable scenario. I could fight, use Light, strategise, withstand pain…but sitting in a classroom talking about hypothetical situations was not the same as lying on the floor of a greater demon's lair. Reality was a harsh wake-up call.

"I was wondering if we'd ever get to see you again."

I bristled at the abrasive voice and slammed my hands over my ears.

"You will look at me when I speak to you," it commanded.

I rolled over, the sound grating in my brain. A man stood over me—tall, ordinary-looking, yet menacing—but I knew he wasn't human. His toothy smile gave him away for one. Rows upon rows of pointy fangs filled the gaping hole that was his mouth, his true form showing through the glamours which hid the Darkness lurking in his perverted meat suit.

It was a Balan, one of the greater demons. It meant I was in huge shite, and that I had zero hope of escape without knowing his true name. I had no power over him without it, but I still had power over myself. It wasn't much considering my repressed self-loathing over my past.

I only hoped I could hold on but I wasn't sure I could even do that.

"The last survivor of Human Convergence." He looked down at me, his lips curling in distaste. "I would like to say you were special, but you weren't. There was no conspiracy. No secret parentage. No otherworldly abilities. You were just a stupid little girl who was in the wrong place at the right time. Any Natural would do. The dumber, the better."

I wasn't the only survivor. There had been others —Jackson and his wife, Esme—so I was hardly alone. Though, I had been the only one to almost succumb to the mutation before it was halted.

"I'm dumb?" I hissed. "I resent that. I'll have you know that I graduated at the top of my class."

His clawed hand wrapped around my throat and

he lifted me off the ground. "Arrogance will be your downfall."

"As will be your rotting meat suit, arsehole."

The Balan growled, his teeth flashing in the torchlight, and I cried out as he poured Darkness into my mind. The intrusion was abrasive, the unfamiliar power tore deep without my Light to stop it.

Reality fell away.

Then…

The sound of water dripping roused me.

I was in the female locker room at the Academy. Laughter echoed off the white tiles and I turned. Kayla, the perfect blonde princess stood in front of the basins, preening herself in the mirror. She was flanked by Trisha and Maisy, her two little hangers-on.

My tormentor and her apprentices. These people defined my adolescence. My personality was bruised and ill-formed because of what they'd put me through.

I stood there, frozen like a lump of dirty black coal. Humiliation and self-loathing poured out of me and I as I took a step backwards, all three girls turned to stare at me.

"Madeleine, there you are," Kayla declared, her eyes complete darkness. "We were wondering when we could get you alone."

"Yeah, Madeleine," Trisha echoed, "we have something important to tell you."

They advanced, forcing me back against the wall. My palms flattened against the tiles and my heart began to beat wildly in my chest.

Kayla lifted her palm and smiled as a flicker of Light played against her skin. "This won't hurt…much."

Before I could react, she slapped me across the face, her power searing my skin. I cried out as pain burned my cheek. Trisha and Maisy began to laugh, egging Kayla on.

She slapped me again, this time on the other cheek.

"You think you can make it as a Natural?" Kayla cried as she tormented me. "A pathetic weirdo like you? You're asking to be possessed, you know that? It was your fault, Madeleine. You let the Dark into the Academy. *You killed us all.*"

Her hand collided with my face, the force of the blow pushing me to the side. Gasping, I stumbled against the row of basins. I caught my reflection and began to shake as I saw the red welts disappear on my face. My Light would heal me, dissolving all the evidence.

No one could help me. Who'd believe the queen bee of the Academy was capable of physical and psychological abuse? No one.

I felt sick and as I stared at myself, reality began to ripple. It hadn't happened like this, but it was close enough.

My gaze met Kayla's in the mirror and she smirked.

"Why don't you just end it," she purred. "No one will miss you, Madeleine. No one at all."

"This isn't real!" I shouted with all my strength. The mirror cracked and I turned to face my demon, pushing her back against the wall. "You're not real!"

The Balan roared his frustration and shook me as the cave came back into focus.

"Did you think you could just dangle me over your creepy blood graffiti, and I'd crack under the insults of a teenage girl?" I mocked. "You will have to try harder than that, *moron*."

The demon growled and let go of my neck, shoving me to the floor. I landed hard, the rock colliding with my knees. Nothing happened for a moment, then pain shot through my legs, taking my breath away.

"Do you want my little ball of mutant Darkness?" I mocked. "Do you want to hold it and comb its hair and tell it you love it?"

The Balan roared at me and his boot slammed into my stomach. I held onto my cry of pain, curling in on myself.

"You kick like a girl!" I said. "Like a human, teenage girl with an Instagram addiction!"

Okay, so taunting a greater demon wasn't the best approach, but it was kind of fun…until I lost consciousness.

The festering meat bag was probably right. My arrogance was going to be my downfall.

I didn't know how long I swam in blackness.

My eyes cracked open and the cave came back into focus little by little with each gritty blink. The putrid stench of my own filth mixed with the walk-in closet of husks. As I lay there, I wondered if this was how it was going to end—with me lying on the floor of a rusted cage, my cheek pressed into the gravel, with out of control body odour. *Glamorous.*

I blinked again. A pair of combat boots stood on the other side of the bars, the torchlight flickering off the shiny toes. The rest of the leather was worn—their owner hadn't cared to rub a little polish into them. The laces were undone, one end trailing into a dirty puddle.

"Wakey wakey, pretty Natural."

Something poked my side. I jerked away, my back hitting the bars.

Light played off a sharp, angled jaw, and as my gaze rose, so did my internal alarm. Cold, piercing eyes stared at me, a glint of amusement doing nothing to warm them. He ran his hand over his shaved head and grunted like he wasn't surprised by my reaction but was disappointed in it anyway.

It was the demon-hybrid from *Adrenaline.*

He leaned against the bars and peered at me. "You're a whole bag of trouble, aren't you?"

"Why can you hold my arondight blade?" I rasped.

He shook his head, perplexed. "Of all the things

you could've asked me, that's what you want to know?"

"Why?" I demanded.

"I'm not going to tell you," he replied. "Ask something a little smarter."

"Why me?"

His lips quirked. "Now we're getting somewhere, but if we're being truthful, you already know why."

Nauseated, I curled in on myself. *The residual demonic mutation…*

"You're a hard nut to crack, pretty Natural," he told me. "That bastard will drill into your mind until you break and when you do…" He drew his finger along his neck. "But I don't have to tell you, do I?"

What was their game plan? Was it to break me, reprogram my mutation to flare again, then send me back to Camelot as a glorified suicide bomber? Or was it to be a spy? They'd been evicted rather abruptly—perhaps they *had* left something important behind.

"What's at Camelot?" I asked, my voice wavering. "What do *you* want?"

The man's eyes flashed silver and he grinned, reminding me what he was. Despite his handsome and extremely human face, I couldn't forget his true nature.

"Well?" I prodded.

"I can get you out of here, but you have to make a deal with me first."

I narrowed my eyes. Making a deal with a demon was bad news, but I was out of options. No

Light and no arondight blade meant no escape. I couldn't crack the lock on this rusty bucket, and even if I did, I wasn't getting five metres without collapsing.

"What do you want?" I hissed.

He knelt and wrapped his hands around the bars. I watched him closely as his cocky demonic expression melted away and took on a human vulnerability.

"No tricks," I snapped.

"No tricks," he echoed. "Listen carefully. The moment you leave this cage, they will know and it's over for the both of us. But not if you do as I say…"

I wanted to trust him, but every bone in my body —the bones that'd been trained to fight his kind since I was a child—screamed at me to run in the other direction. "Why are you helping me?"

"Because you might be able to help me."

Help him? I frowned, the motion causing my head to throb. Help him with what?

I swallowed hard. "How do I get past them?"

He reached through the bars. "You need to take my hand and trust me."

I stared at his outstretched fingers.

"I can help you, but only if I take you under my protection," he urged. "Link with me and you'll see."

"Link with you?" My mouth fell open. "I can't… I—"

"I know you can feel it," he said, his voice low. "It's the only thing keeping you alive…and it's the only thing that will set you free."

"I don't believe you." My demon mutation was

going to save my life? This was a trick. A manipulation. "Get out of my head."

"This is real," the man hissed, "and we need to go now."

I closed my eyes. The risk was too great, but I didn't have any other choice. If I stayed here, the greater demon would dismantle my mind piece by piece and drive me mad, before a long agonising death. If I went with the man—the hybrid—I had a chance to escape back to Camelot.

Opening my eyes, I lifted my hand. It was the lesser of two shitty options. My fingertips brushed against his and I felt power flare into my body through his touch. I lurched forwards, pulled by an unseen force and his hand wrapped around my wrist.

He pulled me to my feet and I passed through the bars, the metal shimmering as if it'd been an illusion all along. Gasping, I fell against the man's chest. His arms circled around me, holding me upright as my knees trembled.

I couldn't remember how long had it been since someone had held me like this?

"I've got you," the man murmured. "Stay close, pretty Natural, and don't let go."

What had I done? Had I unknowingly sold him my soul? Confusion began to take over—I didn't even know what he wanted from me. I pushed against him, dislodging his grasp, and fell against the bars, which had become solid once more.

Movement at the cave entrance drew my gaze and I froze as a demon slunk through the jagged opening.

Its slimy black arms flopped back and forth, and its claws scratched the limestone underfoot as it approached. It took one look at me and bared its pointed teeth.

"What the hell is going on here?" Its voice was surprisingly human, but the sound grated against my mind like sandpaper.

The man turned as I clapped my hands over my ears.

The demon seemed furious, but I couldn't tell through the pounding. "When he finds out——"

The man moved fast, lunging towards the demon and fisting his hand into the creature's straggly hair. With one fluid motion, he slammed its head into the wall, the crack of splintering bone echoed off stone.

"He's not going to find out," the man snarled as the lifeless body slid to the ground.

Then he turned towards me. His eyes were two pits of blackness, and I began to regret my decision.

"Your demon is showing," I told him as my hands slipped away from my ears.

He shook his head, the motion seeming to clear the unyielding darkness, and his gaze returned to normal. Holding out his hand, he gestured for me. "I told you not to let go."

Reluctantly, I slipped my hand into his and he tugged me close.

It turned out that the cave was actually part of a larger complex of tunnels and caverns. We emerged from my alcove into a massive cavern, then into a side tunnel before finding another larger room.

I knew little about rocks and formations, but I knew about stalagmites and stalactites. Massive points dangled from the ceiling, their partners reaching up out of the gloom towards them. The faint dripping sound of their ancient growth echoed as we waited.

"Why have we stopped?" I whispered.

"*Shh*," the man hissed. His grip tightened and a moment later, a ripple ebbed through me, its source unknown.

I looked at him but he didn't acknowledge me. Once the cave had settled, he urged me down another twisting tunnel.

The ground was smooth, worn by the constant tramping of footsteps. I gathered we must be near the exit, which meant the chance of discovery was at an all-time high.

I looked over my shoulder and for a split-second, the dank cave shimmered and another existence radiated through a veil of Darkness. My eyes widened at the exposed world hidden underground.

The walls were polished to a smooth obsidian, and from within the glossy surface, eyes peered back at me. Carvings. Skulls, death, twisted gods—who knew what demons liked to decorate their hidden lairs with. Torches hung at regular intervals along the tunnel— points of red flame suspended in midair with nothing to hold them aloft.

"Don't look back," the man said as he pulled me along the tunnel.

Cold air blasted my skin and I gasped as the wind

took my breath away, along with the imposing despair the cave had pressed down on me.

Overhead, the stars shone between patches of clouds. The moon was almost full, its light illuminating the icy vista before us.

The man let go of my hand and turned towards the side of the cliff where a path had been carved into the solid rock.

"Can you manage it?" he asked.

I felt warmth pulse through my veins as Light began to ease into my body. Whatever had dampened my power was gone. I was free.

I flexed my fingers and the throb in my head began to ease. "Yes."

The man nodded in understanding and began to move. He intended to lead me down the mountain, and I was glad.

"Hey, I don't even know your name," I said, the wind tearing at my hair.

He turned, his mouth pulling up to one side. The grin made him look roguish in the murky light and my insides fluttered.

"Elijah," he said. "My name is Elijah."

6

I waited in a bush while Elijah secured us a cottage in a budget campground.

The cave they had locked me up in was a few miles from Ben Nevis, a mountain in the Scottish Highlands. If anyone had been searching for me at Camelot, they'd be looking in the wrong place. We were four-hundred miles away, in a twist I hadn't seen coming.

Honestly, this wasn't one of my smarter moves. I was putting my trust into a demon. A *demon*. This was unprecedented. I'd never heard of anyone crossing enemy lines and *making friends*. Bloody hell. If I wasn't going to get thrown out of the Sanctum before, I was now.

I could see Elijah through the window of the small stone reception cottage, talking to an employee. He looked human enough, but he could turn on the scary demonic stuff without even thinking about it.

I had so many questions.

Turning my gaze onto the path, I scanned the campground. A few cabins seemed to be occupied, but other than that, there wasn't any movement. This time of year, it was far too cold to pitch a tent. At least nothing had followed us down from the mountain…yet.

I never knew how evolved the Dark had become. The truth of those caves had been hidden from me, but when I'd looked back… How many underground networks did they have? The walls had been smooth and constructed with care, and there were carvings which denoted intelligence beyond the need to consume.

Cut off from the One, demon-kind had created its own civilisation. They were gathering as one, rebuilding. And once they had, who knew what they'd do?

I had to get back to Camelot and warn the others.

"Madeleine."

Elijah materialised out of thin air, peering at me behind the bush. I must look real put together right about now.

I hesitated—the sound of his voice soothing yet chilling at the same time. "H-How do you know my name?"

"I know a lot about you."

"How?"

He glanced over his shoulder. "We better go inside. It's cold out."

"Why did you help me?"

"They gave us a cottage at the far end," he said, ignoring me. "C'mon."

Short of hot-wiring a car, I didn't have a way out of here, so I followed—rather reluctantly, I might add.

The cabin was tiny. A kitchen with a dining table big enough for two joined into a small living area with a hideous floral couch, two matching armchairs, and a television. Two doors led to more rooms—a bedroom and a bathroom—but that was it.

"You need to start talking," I demanded as soon as the door closed.

Elijah rolled his eyes and folded his long limbs into the armchair. "You're really bossy, you know that?"

"If you won't tell me, I'm leaving." I strode towards the door but barely made it halfway across the room before he yanked me backwards.

I fell onto the couch with a cry and rolled onto the floor. Landing on my knees, I scowled at Elijah, who was still sitting in the armchair. He hadn't moved an inch.

"What have you done?" I demanded.

"I told you…" he replied with a smirk. "You're the one who chose not to listen."

Link with me… I cried out in frustration. He was right, the son of a—

"You bound me to you?" I exclaimed. "Arsehole!"

Elijah shrugged. "I had to make sure you'd hold up your end of the bargain."

"You tricked me!"

"I didn't trick you," he argued. "I just omitted a few details."

"That's the same thing!"

"You really need to lower your voice." He stood and walked the two steps to the bathroom and opened the door, then turned on the light. "You want a shower? You smell."

He was so irritating. I vaulted over the couch, grabbed the door handle, and slammed it closed.

Nausea spread through me and I winced. He was tugging at the link. "Stop it."

"Just making sure you're still there." He smirked, pleased with himself.

"Why did you kill that demon?" I demanded, deciding to start small. "The one at the club. You had no reason to help me."

"It was a Wanderer."

I frowned, not understanding. "Wanderer?"

"For all your prowess, you Naturals never knew much, did you? Still don't."

"If you won't tell me what it was, then why did you kill it?"

"It was in my way."

"Your way of what?"

"I can see beauty and intelligence aren't mutual concepts. How disappointing."

"You're really mean, you know that?"

"I am a demon, or have you forgotten?" he scoffed at me. "You Naturals are all the same…just a bunch of arrogant arseholes."

"*Bullshit.*"

"Your Twin Flames were nothing but a fluke," he went on. "The Druids didn't know what they were doing either. They saw a lost cause and did the smart thing…they left."

"Was not," I argued. "The Druids were hunted by —" Wait. How did he know these things? I thought he was a hybrid like I'd been—a human mutated by Human Convergence.

Elijah looked at me, his eyes flashing silver in the muted light.

I tensed and flattened my back against the wall. "You're a greater demon."

He snorted. "Hardly."

His gaze raked over me and despite myself, my heart fluttered. I could think of at least ten regulations I'd broken just by standing here. Wilder was going to blow a fuse when he found out. Scratch that last and make it *if* he found out.

"Tired?" Elijah asked.

I swallowed hard. "What?"

"Your Light holds back the pain, but the more you struggle, the worse your injuries will get."

"Shows how much you know," I drawled. "Given enough time, my Light heals me. *It's been enough time.*"

He snorted and took a step towards me. "Have you been seriously injured since your Light returned?"

"I—" I thought about my final months of training at the Academy and the years I'd spent patrolling London. Apart from some bumps and bruises, I'd never been to the infirmary for anything other than routine check-ups.

"If you're so sure, then let go of your Light."

I was never one to back down from a challenge.

Call me stubborn—or arrogant as everyone liked to tell me—but I wasn't about to lose face in front of a demon, no matter how hot his outsides were.

"Fine," I spat.

The effect was instantaneous. My knees buckled as the full force of pain I'd been holding back hit every nerve ending in my body. Elijah caught me before I hit the floor, sliding his arms underneath mine.

"See?" he murmured.

I was shaking. "I don't understand…"

He eased me back onto the couch. "That little ball of demonic energy hiding inside you is to blame."

"I never knew it was there," I murmured. "How could…"

"I've been asking myself the same thing."

My head throbbed. "Something else is going on here."

Elijah raised his eyebrows. "Is that a question or a statement?"

"Both."

He shook his head and picked up the throw blanket from the back of the couch. "Think about it," he said, draping it over me. "You have all the pieces."

I let my Light flow back into my limbs and as the pain subsided, I thought about his mysterious 'pieces'. At *Adrenaline*, the demon—or the Wanderer as he'd called it—had led me into the crowded club only to attack and almost reveal me to the humans. Elijah had saved me, only to lead me outside and away from the scene. *He led me away.* What did he do next? He'd helped me escape from the Balan.

Now I was lying on a couch in a cottage in the middle of the Scottish Highlands, with a demon who'd just put blanket over me. It was feeling like a perverted doctor-patient fantasy.

Then there were the demons who had attacked me and Trent. They'd said *she knows it.* She knows it, like I already knew why they were there.

My gaze met Elijah's. "They were looking for me from the start. At the club, you… They were going to take me then."

He nodded. "And now you're free, they will try again."

"But I'm not special, I—"

His eyes flashed silver. "Stop underselling yourself. It's irritating."

I shook my head, though my temples still throbbed. There as only one reason I could think of why they'd want me. "That Balan wants to bring back Human Convergence?"

"I'm not sure. It could be many things."

I narrowed my eyes. So far, Elijah had done nothing but protect me from the Dark, but he was one of them. His motives were cloudy at best, yet here I was. "And where do you fit in with all this? What am I to you?"

"You were mutated," he stated.

"Thanks for the reminder. It's not like I'd prefer to forget that time in my life or anything."

"And now you're not," he finished his earlier thought. "How?"

"We were cured when Mordred was vanquished," I told him. I had no problems telling him—it was common knowledge.

Elijah's expression fell. "Your people researched the program. They must've found out something. They…"

My revelation seemed to have thrown him and finally, I understood what he wanted from me, because he *was* me. Elijah was a demon-hybrid looking for a way out.

"You're looking for a way to cure yourself."

Something was different about his mutation. He wasn't a part of Human Convergence…not like I'd been. A different strain ran through his body, but where had it originated from? Had someone reopened the project?

"Elijah?"

His expression twisted and he grabbed me around the throat. "If you tell them about me, I'll kill you myself."

It was then that I realised there were two halves of him. One light and one dark, both in constant struggle to dominate. It'd only been a few hours since he'd busted me out of that cage, but I had already noted the times when he'd been gentle, and those times when his mood seemed to have snapped a complete one-eighty to arseholeville.

Now I understood why he'd sought me out. Elijah

thought I'd been through the same thing and conquered it.

But I hadn't…

There hadn't been one second that I'd been able to switch between two different sides of myself. The mutation had been in control, only allowing me to come out when it wanted to remain hidden—there was never a choice. In the end, it was only Scarlett who'd been able to stop it from taking over entirely.

I gasped as his fingers bit into my skin. "Elijah. *Stop*."

"What that Balan did in the cave will pale compared to what I do to you."

My vision began to explode with black spots, and I pushed a burst of Light through my body into Elijah's hands.

He grunted as my power zapped him, the air cracking as if he'd brushed up against a live electrical wire. His grasp loosened and he fell to his knees, his shoulders shaking with silent sobs.

I sat up, the blanket falling away. "Elijah?"

"Can you see now?" he whispered.

I nodded. "I can see."

The Dark wanted to make me turn again and use the remnants of my mutation for unknown ends. Elijah simply wanted my help and had bound himself to me to make sure I'd follow through. His allegiance to either side was muddy at best, but I was stuck with him until he decided to let me go.

Whatever I chose next—or was forced to do—

would put me in a precarious position with Wilder and the Regula.

"You've put me in an impossible position," I said, kneeling in front of Elijah.

My heart thrummed a wild rhythm. I remembered how easily he crushed the skull of that demon back in the cave and swallowed hard. There was nothing to stop him from doing the same to me, but something unspoken said I could trust him. Well, at least as far as not killing me went.

"I still remember what it was like…" he whispered, lost in some memory, "before they took me."

I reached out and took his hand, unafraid. When our skin met, an image flashed in my mind, transported by Elijah's link.

A wild, overgrown forest. A ring of standing stones. Smoke from a campfire. Bare feet dangling in a stream. The rest was blood.

I wasn't sure he meant for me to see it, but I did. How much had he lost at the hands of the Dark? What had they made him do?

"Wait…" I drew my hand away. "How long have you been like this?"

His lips curved into a grimace. "A while."

Elijah wouldn't tell me any more. After he'd composed himself, he was back to being a complete smart arse, but at least I knew the deal between us.

There were gaping holes in his story and a whole heap of unanswered questions, but it was a start.

I slept through the last hours of the night, and when the sun rose, I dragged myself into the shower. Despite knowing the Balan's visions were bogus, I checked my reflection. My face was fine.

Elijah was waiting for me when I emerged in a waft of steam. My clothes were still caked in mud and Light knew what else, but at least the stench had lessened.

His feet were kicked up onto the dining table and the chair leaned back precariously on two legs. The worlds 'effortless arsehole' came to mind.

In the daylight, he looked totally different. He still had his menacing disposition, but it was as if I was looking at him for the first time. His eyes still kept their silver sheen, but beyond the veil, they were a steely blue, almost like a stormy tropical ocean.

In that moment, I was agonisingly aware that at his core, Elijah was a man—the feeling was unsettling and totally foreign.

"We can wait until you're fully healed or we can go now," he said, unaware of the internal dilemma going on inside me. "It's your choice, but I thought you'd want to keep your demonic, whatever that thing is, a secret."

He was right, but I wasn't about to admit it. I didn't want anyone to know I might still harbour a mutation after the things I'd done.

"I'm feeling much better," I said. "It'll take me a

few hours to get back to Camelot, so I suspect the last few bruises will be gone by then."

He cocked an eyebrow. "You?"

I stared at him and shrugged. "I know how to drive a car."

"That's nice, but I'm taking you," he stated. "I have to make sure you get there in one piece."

I rolled my eyes. "And here I thought you just longed for my company." He tugged on the invisible link between us and I coughed. "That's going to wear real thin, real fast."

"I thought you might want to go," he declared, kicking his boots off the table. "While you were shaving your legs, the neighbour was nice enough to loan us his car." He took out a set of keys from his jacket pocket and began to twirl them around his finger.

It was my turn to raise my eyebrows. "And by loan, you mean stole?"

"You Naturals manipulate things out of humans all the time. Don't think I don't know all your tricks."

"Can Darkness do that?" I wondered. Demons could influence humans, but only subtly. When they wanted more direct control, that's where possession came into play. Elijah couldn't possess anyone, but he had Darkness at his disposal thanks to his mutation.

He began to look bored and I was wondering if it was his way of avoiding questions he didn't want to answer. "Alteration, manipulation, mind control—it's all the same thing."

"So, what happens if I tell my boss about you?"

His eyes sparkled as he laughed. "You won't."

"You sound so sure."

Elijah rose to his feet. "If there's one thing I know about you, Madeline Greenbriar, it's that you're loyal…to a fault."

I didn't like it when he said my name, but I was just telling myself that to make myself feel better. It was creepy, yet kind of alluring. I was so weird.

The front door opened and he walked out, leaving me standing in the cottage.

"If we hurry, I can get you back to your crumbling castle by bedtime." His voice echoed around me. "Or you can wait here for your friends in the mountain to collect you."

I yelped and scurried after him, wondering if I was choosing the lesser of two evils. The only way to know was to let Elijah's game play out.

7

———

The car Elijah had 'borrowed' was a slate grey Jaguar F-Pace—a forty-thousand-pound luxury SUV. The leather seats were so soft, I caught myself stroking them once too often. It was way posh. There was an eight-inch touchscreen in the dash that gave all kinds of stats about the car, along with navigation and music, and little buttons that controlled the heating and cooling…and the seat warmers.

Elijah slapped my hand away from the screen with an annoyed sigh. "Stop it. You're like a child."

"I've never seen a car like this before." I rubbed my knuckles as the Scottish Highlands flashed past and glared at the demon behind the wheel.

"It's the twenty-first century," he scoffed.

"So?" I stuck my tongue out at him and settled back into the seat.

"I would've thought you would have utilised technology to win the war."

"Technology makes us weak."

"I'll never understand you Naturals."

"I'll never understand you…whatever it is you like to call yourself."

"There's no one else like me," he revealed, "so I wouldn't know."

I raised my eyebrows and studied his profile. No one else like him, huh? That was good news—it meant Human Convergence hadn't fired back up to its previous production levels.

Elijah's expression revealed nothing else, so I turned back to the window, watching the wild landscape change as we descended from the Highlands.

Scotland was beautiful. I preferred the city, but there was something about the untamable wilderness at the top of the world that tugged at my heartstrings.

"We're being followed." Elijah's voice snapped me out of my daydream.

"Really?"

"Yes, really. I can sense them."

"Who are they? The same arseholes who captured me?"

"It seems like it."

I shook my head in disbelief. "Those things can drive a car? Have you seen their nails? I can't believe how they get through life without having to clip them."

Elijah snorted. "How did you people ever survive?"

"With—"

"That was a rhetorical question." He glanced in the rearview mirror. "Do you know what rhetorical means?"

"It's a question that doesn't require an answer."

"*Exactly*." What a complete a-hole.

"How many?" I asked.

"Two."

"What are they driving?"

"A Volkswagen Polo."

I snorted, almost choking on my spit, then burst into laughter. "Demons are following us in a Volkswagen Polo? *Seriously*?"

"They're not good at selecting cars, but it's not funny," he barked at me. "It won't stop them from killing me and taking you."

"Can we outrun them?" I asked, wiping at my tears.

"Yes, but that would be a bad idea. Best to kill them before they give away our position."

"I don't have my arondight blade," I told him. "We'll have to lose them and cover our tracks somehow."

His hands tightened around the steering wheel. "You rely on your weapons too much."

"How else am I supposed to kill demons?" I demanded. "I can't slice off their heads with my resting bitch face, you know."

"You kill them with your Light."

"My Light? It's not strong enough to take down a demon. That's what my sword is for."

Elijah sighed. "You're really starting to irritate me."

"Excuse me?" I huffed. "If I'm so annoying, then why bother saving me at all? You seem pretty comfortable being a demon. Were those tears just for show last night?"

He growled and slammed his fist down on the steering wheel. "*Bitch.*"

"Your demon is showing again." I smirked and looked back at the car behind us.

As if he was taunting me, Elijah pressed the button to kill the ignition and the engine died. We began to coast down the road, sailing around the bend.

I tensed as we began to slow. "What are you doing?"

"I can't let them live," he replied. "Sword or no sword, we will fight."

I supposed I had to agree with him. If the Dark found out he'd helped me escape, he was dead— regardless of his allegiance to them. Considering I was bound to the guy who knew what that meant for me, I seriously hoped this wasn't one of those 'I get hurt so you get hurt' scenarios.

Besides, I didn't want to go back so we were still on the same page…for now.

"But it's broad daylight," I argued.

Elijah scoffed. "Demons aren't vampires, Madeleine. We can withstand direct sunlight."

"That's not what I meant. What if a human comes along and sees us?"

"We'll be cloaked."

"Until a car crashes into an invisible Volkswagen Polo!"

He smirked at me, his lips pulling up on one side. "We better make it quick, then."

The handbrake ratcheted on and the car jerked to a halt. Behind us, the Polo stopped five car lengths up a gradual incline, the rear end was obscured by a raggedy box hedge.

Elijah threw open the door and stepped out onto the road like the cocky bastard he was. Sighing, I clambered out of the passenger seat and followed him.

Cool air brushed against my skin as we stood together, waiting for the demons to make their move, but they stayed put in the Polo.

"They're not getting out," I said.

"Obviously," Elijah drawled. "They're just confused."

"Or calling for back-up."

"Unlikely."

"How do you know?" I demanded and glared at him.

"You're really asking me that question?"

"Yeah, you're a demon, but that answer is a cop out. How do you know?"

He grunted and began to walk towards the Volkswagen. I guess that was as good an answer as I was going to get.

I threw up my hand, more to check if we were concealed than anything, and followed him. Knowing

I was about to fight without my arondight blade felt as if I'd lost a limb, but there was nothing I could do about it.

Elijah was right. They had to die, and if he was right about my Light… Well, that was another can of worms I'd have to deal with—*if it was opened.*

The front doors of the Polo opened as we approached, and two slimy black demons slid out. Not concerned their birthday suits were showing, they lopped towards us, their tongues darting between their thin lips like a slithering snake.

Man, every time I saw one of these things, they creeped me the hell out. I couldn't imagine what they used to be before the rift was closed—seven-foot-tall walls of rubbery black muscle, snappy teeth, and razor-sharp claws. I couldn't believe Scarlett had fought these and lived, but then again, she was the living embodiment of Arondight—and Arondight could do just about anything.

I allowed my Light to flare, hoping my meagre power had at least enough zap to take down one of these things in their weakened state.

Elijah edged towards the creature on the right, leaving the other to me.

"Okay, no sword," I muttered. "I've got this."

The demon lunged and I dodged to the side. Twisting, I struck its back with a burst of Light, but it merely stumbled as if I had jostled it.

I cursed and tried again before it could regain its footing. The heel of my boot collided with its ribs, but the creature was too quick. Claws wrapped around my ankle and the demon pulled. My knee buckled and I landed on the flat of my back with an angry grunt.

I rolled to the side as claws rushed towards my face, then back as its other hand struck. Both sets slammed into asphalt, cracking the surface of the road. And here I was thinking they wanted to capture me alive. What a fool I was!

The demon pinned me under its slimy body, trapping me in its grasp. I pushed my lower half off the ground and kicked upwards with both feet. The soles of my boots slammed into its gut and I added a pulse of Light which sent the creature flying. I flipped, landing on my feet, and raised my fists.

I turned to check on Elijah, but he was doing fine. His hand was grasped around the other demon's neck, his Darkness searing through flesh. What was he trying to do? Squeeze its head off?

His gaze met mine. "*Madeleine.*"

I swung back just as the demon I'd sent rolling down the road came at me with incredible speed. We collided, the impact jarring my body.

Unfortunately, I landed on my back again with it straddling me. This was getting embarrassing.

I slammed my palms against the demon's head, the strength in my arms the only thing stopping it from eating my face off. Struggling against it, I sent pulse after pulse of Light into its brain, but it wasn't enough to bring it down.

"Just. *Die!*" I screamed at it, the limits of my power beginning to flicker.

Dammit, I needed my sword!

"Elijah!" I shouted.

A boot collided with the demon's ribs and it rolled down the road. Elijah leapt over me, not even stopping, and tore into the demon like it was putty in his hands.

Turning away from the carnage, I breathed deeply. Sucking in a lungful of sulphuric air, I gagged. Slick, congealed black blood—and other juicy things —coated the road. Elijah had torn the demon apart like a savage beast.

I must never forget what he is…

A shadow loomed over me, and sensing Elijah, I looked up at him.

"I should have left you in the car," he drawled, glaring at me. He didn't even bother to offer me his hand, so I was left to stand on my own.

"And I told you I needed my sword!"

"No, you don't."

"Yes, I do."

"No, you don't."

"Yes, I do!"

"No, *you don't.*"

"We will be here all day if you keep that up," I snarled.

"Your Light is meant to protect the innocent," he said, looking down at the dismembered demon. "A sword is merely a tool."

"But we've never been able to do that. Light doesn't vanquish the Dark."

Elijah rolled his eyes. "Light and shadow, night

and day. *Whatever.* You're a good warrior, Madeline, but you could be great if you just got over yourself and opened your mind."

"I can't change biology," I argued. "And I can't change the laws of physics."

"You can."

"But—"

"Things are different now. The Dark is evolving to survive. It's not a simple fight for balance anymore. You're so worried about the things you can't do, you're blind to the things you *can*."

"Why do you care so much?" I exclaimed. "If I don't get your cure, I'm toast, and if I do, you're gone... Why does any of this even matter?"

He levelled his gaze at me. "You stupid girl."

I sucked in a sharp breath. One second he was making me swoon, the next he was a condescending prick. Talk about extreme whiplash.

He snorted, irritated at my stunned silence, and began to walk towards the Polo. I was slow on the uptake and I grimaced in annoyance.

My mutation evolved to survive.

I followed him up the road, my cheeks red with embarrassment, helping him roll the car off the road and into the field. The police would chalk it up to an abandoned stolen vehicle. The bodies however...

I walked back down the road, but I frowned when I stood over the first demon. It was bubbling like hot tar in the sunlight. It's black eyeball popped and I jumped out of the splatter zone.

"Leave it," Elijah said, striding past me.

"But—"

"They will be gone in five minutes. Ten at the most."

Getting a whiff of decaying fart gas, I curled my nose and jogged after him. This was one thing I wasn't going to argue about.

When we returned to the Jaguar, I'd barely closed the door when Elijah stepped on the accelerator. I didn't have it in me to chew him out over it—not after I had witnessed his fighting style.

The car tore off down the lonely road, back on its path south.

We arrived at Camelot just after sunset.

Road-tripping with a demon-hybrid hadn't been on the top of my bucket list, but all things considered, eight hours in a stolen car with Elijah wasn't that bad.

As we left the road behind and climbed the hill, I thought over my predicament. Bound to a demon-hybrid, hunted by a Balan, and still harbouring my mutation. That wasn't even counting the precarious ground I stood on with the Regula.

I had to help Elijah. As long as I was bound to him, he'd protect me from the Balan, and searching for his cure might help with ridding me of my own internal issues. What other choice did I have?

Reaching the rise, we looked down at Camelot and I shivered. The lights of base camp filtered through the veil, warm and inviting after being stuffed in a cage.

"How does this link work?" I asked.

Elijah seemed to hesitate beside me, his expression troubled. He probably thought I was going to screw him over, though he'd all but insured I wouldn't. Revealing his existence would reveal mine.

He glanced at me. "The farther apart we are, the less physical control I'm able to exert."

"That's reassuring."

"But I'll always know where you are."

I sighed. "And that's less reassuring."

"They can't know about me," he said. "If your people find me…" he trailed off, but I understood his meaning. The Dark was using him, but the Light would want to cut him apart and figure out how he worked.

"They would help you," I started slowly. "Ramona is an excellent doctor. She stopped my mutation from progressing after Scarlett brought back my soul. Hey, maybe Arondight could help you? And Jackson is developing technology to—"

"You're one of them, Madeleine," Elijah interrupted. "They'd help *you*, regardless."

"But you're an innocent."

He shook his head. "You better go."

I nodded and began to make my way down the hill. I felt his gaze on my back, burning into my flesh. He was just letting me go? Surely there was a failsafe in his plan other than letting his demon side hunt me down. What was the catch?

Maybe he saw something in me I didn't. I had an overwhelming urge to run back up the hill to persuade him to come with me.

But when I turned for one last glimpse, Elijah was already gone.

8

———

I strode through base camp and ignored the stunned looks as I walked towards the security tent.

"We've searched every inch of these bloody hills and there's no sign of her." Thompson's voice filtered through the gap and I paused.

"She can't have just disappeared into thin air." *Aiden*.

"Those demons took her. I saw it with my own eyes." Trent's voice joined the argument. "They were just like the creatures Scarlett said she fought when she went back in time. They were much smaller, but I could hardly stand against one, let alone two. Madeleine had three on her."

"She's been gone three days," Thompson said. "She could be anywhere by now. We have to face facts."

"Face facts?" Trent shouted. "You're giving up on her?"

"No one's giving up on anybody," Aiden replied calmly. "We need to contact the field offices in Edinburgh and Cardiff. We'll have to inform the London Sanctum. Her parents—"

"Are on a deep cover operation," Thompson snapped. "Madeleine has trained for this...we all have. She's on her own."

I scoffed. Seriously? Thompson was giving up on me after three days? That was hardly anything, but he was right—I trained for this. But if it hadn't been for Elijah, I wasn't sure I would've been able to get out of that cage on my own. At least not right away. *You keep telling yourself that, Madeleine.*

I lifted my hand and went to push the flap aside and make my grand entrance, but I hesitated. Did I belong here? It didn't matter. Elijah needed a cure and I was stuck to him like superglue.

I gritted my teeth and stormed into the tent. All eyes turned towards my abrupt entrance and I scowled at Thompson. "*She's on her own?*"

"Madeleine!" Trent exclaimed.

"You better thank the bloody Light I got out of that stinking cage, Thompson, otherwise—"

Trent threw his arms around my neck, cutting off my tirade before I could insult my superior officer further. "I thought they'd killed you. When you fell—"

"Yeah, yeah," I said, awkwardly brushing him away.

"Madeleine, thank the Light," Aiden said as he grasped my arm. "What happened to you?"

"Where do you want me to start?" I asked.

"There's the bit where I was locked in a cage at the back of a greater demon's meat closet. They took my Light and busted me up real good. Oh, and there was the bit where they tried to mentally torture me with visions of high school bullying. Then there was the hidden compound in a cave system underneath Ben Nevis. I had to climb down the side of the bloody mountain in the dark, I'll have you know. I'm *so* not a mountaineer." They stared at me with wide eyes as I blurted out a severely lacking version of my ordeal. It had all the key points, though. "But thanks for giving up on me, Thompson. Real cute."

His eyes narrowed, not liking my challenge. "You know the protocol for these situations, Madeline."

My little internal friend flared and now that I was aware of it, I wondered if it was responsible for my bitchy attitude. Wouldn't that be a copout? "When I became a warrior, I wanted to be part of something greater than myself, but no one told me it meant I'd be demoted to just a number."

"*Madeleine—*"

"Caleb," Aiden interrupted, "there's a time and place for this. And it is not now." He turned to me, his expression kind. Out of the two brothers, I knew which I preferred. "We best get you some clean clothes and a warm bed."

"They're organising themselves," I said, glaring at the arsehole brother. "They're coming together and creating a community. I saw it. The creatures who escaped Camelot are being led by a greater demon— a Balan. They're moving away from their need to consume…it's like they're evolving into a new species to survive."

The men stared at me for a moment, not knowing what to say. Trent coughed, looking worried.

"This is bad," Aiden said quietly after a moment of internal deliberation. "If the Dark is congregating and evolving without the One, then another war could erupt."

The last gasp. I'd told Trent about it, and no one else seem concerned. Without a master, the Naturals had believed the demons would scatter and eventually die out, but I'd seen otherwise.

"But why Madeline?" Thompson mused. "Why take her and not Trent?"

I coughed, almost choking on my spit. "Camelot," I blurted. "They're interested in Camelot."

"What on Earth could they want here?" Aiden mused. "There are no energy signatures or hidden pockets of time, and the rift is sealed. That entire area is dead."

I shrugged. "I suggest you keep digging, then."

An awkward silence fell on the tent. After a long moment, Aiden coughed and gestured at me. "Let's get you to the infirmary. Ramona will want to check you out herself."

My heart leapt. "Ramona's here?"

"She arrived yesterday," Aiden explained, then to Trent, he said, "Can you escort Madeleine?"

They most likely wanted to talk about my revelations. I bristled, not enjoying being left out.

"C'mon," Trent said, urging me towards the door, "you kinda stink."

"Wow," I drawled. "*Welcome home.*"

He chuckled and held open the tent flap for me. The moment it fell back into place, I could hear the Thompsons start to argue. They really needed to check their volume.

The infirmary was empty when we arrived. Given the late hour, and it was past dinnertime, everyone was elsewhere doing whatever archaeology nerds did for fun.

Ramona was bent over a workstation, her auburn hair pulled back into a severe braid. She was in her late thirties, intelligent, bordering on six foot tall, and had been the head of the medical and science team at the London Sanctum for almost ten years. She was a notorious raging workaholic, so it didn't surprise me to see her taking over for the poor soul who had been rostered on for emergency duty that night.

Ramona was also the only person who could successfully pull me up on my bullshit, which made my current situation kind of awkward.

She looked up upon our entrance. "Madeline!" She dropped what she was doing and crossed the tent, drawing me in for a hug despite Trent's earlier stench assessment. "When did you—"

"She just burst in out of nowhere," Trent told her.

"Handling shite on her own, just like she always does."

I sighed, inhaling the lemony fresh scent of her oversized black sweater. "I don't know whether to be insulted or not."

Ramona drew back and clucked her tongue at him before shooing him away. "Off with you, Trent. Leave us women in peace."

I gave him a look and all he could do was shrug as he scurried away. He knew what was good for him.

"So, I gather you don't want to talk about it?" Ramona asked as she forced me to sit on the end of an empty bed.

"You gather right." I looked around the tent. It was immaculate, having only seen the odd bump and bruise from Naturals on the dig site. "What are you doing at Camelot? It doesn't seem like the hive of activity you'd be interested in."

She snorted and began her examination, checking my eyes before moving to make sure I had no gaping wounds or broken bones my Light should've healed. Thankfully, I'd been right about the last bruises healing before Elijah dropped me off.

"Things are quiet," she replied. "Esme has things handled, and Jackson is busy in his laboratory these days. I figured I'd come see the famous Camelot myself."

"And what's the verdict?"

She clucked her tongue. "I didn't think it'd be this chaotic."

I smirked. "You're welcome."

I fell silent, letting Ramona go through the motions. It was more for her benefit than mine—I felt completely fine, though my mind was pulled in all kinds of directions. I already felt a change inside me. I didn't know what it was—a chemical imbalance, a revelation, a spiritual alignment—but something was going on and I was convinced it had to do with a certain arsehole.

Within five minutes of being bound, Elijah had challenged me like no one else had. He forced me to think, to push my boundaries, and—*dare I say it*—to grow up.

I also knew nothing about him. Where he'd come from, what he'd done, who he was working for, what his motives were, and how long he'd been a demon-hybrid…but despite all the alarm bells, I wanted to help him. Not because he'd bound himself to me, but because when I looked at him, I saw myself.

I shook my head, ridding myself of my irrational thoughts. Maybe I was a stupid little girl.

"Well, your Light seems to have returned and done my job for me," Ramona said. I felt her power brush against mine as she checked for other symptoms and jerked away. "Madeleine?"

"Sorry," I replied.

She frowned but didn't probe any further. "You're not tired?"

I shook my head. "I feel fine."

"Physically, you appear to be completely healthy…"

I narrowed my eyes. "But?"

"Are you sure nothing else happened out there?" she asked quietly as she looked me over. "Because you know you can tell me, Madeleine. We've been through worse than this."

I couldn't tell her about the mutation. If I did, I'd be sent to a lab and put under quarantine. After losing my post at the London Sanctum, I wasn't about to jeopardise my last chance at Camelot. It wasn't like I was going to put anyone in danger and go full Dark again.

But Elijah… I felt his presence tug at me and wondered where he was.

"Did you ever find a way to completely reverse the effects of Human Convergence?" I asked.

Ramona looked thoughtful for a moment. "What sparked this?"

"I, uh… The demon got into my head," I told her. "He made me believe…"

"That your mutation was back?"

"I can't be sure what was real and what was an illusion." I felt a pang as the lie passed my lips.

"Madeleine, you've nothing to worry about," she reassured me. "When Scarlett and Wilder—"

"I know." Except it wasn't gone. "But did you?"

Her frown deepened. "We never had to. When Mordred died—"

I nodded. "I know." But that didn't help Elijah…or me.

Ramona sighed and sat beside me. "You went through a traumatic experience, Madeleine. Anyone would experience echoes after the battering your mind took." She tapped on her tablet and added to my patient notes. "Don't be alarmed, though. We can manage the symptoms."

"Symptoms?"

"It will take a few days for things to settle down. You might experience mild hallucinations, dreams, and other phenomena."

"Hallucinations?" I swallowed hard, suddenly questioning everything that'd happened since the Balan drilled into my mind

Her hand pressed against my shoulder. "Don't worry, we can manage it."

"How much more of this do I have to take?" I whispered. The ex-demon everyone blamed for almost destroying the Academy, captured by demons. It didn't look so good now that I thought about it.

Ramona set the tablet down, hiding her expression before turning towards me. "Madeleine, you're one of the strongest Naturals I've ever known, but you have to give yourself some time."

"For what?"

"To reconcile."

"Screw that. They'll think I've been compromised," I told her. "I've always been on the outer, but now——" My voice broke.

"Madeleine," she placed her hands on my shoulders, "it's not about everyone else. It's about how you choose to react to it."

Or how I chose to handle the thing inside me. I wanted to trust her, but I didn't know what to do about Elijah and his stupid binding. I had to tread carefully, at least for now.

I looked up at Ramona. "I haven't been doing a good job, have I?"

"You're young," she replied, though not unkindly. "And everyone's path is different. But it's up to you where you put your feet."

I lowered my gaze, unsure what to say.

"But enough about that." Ramona patted her hand on the set of clean clothes on the bed. "Let's get you warmed up, huh?"

***

I was ordered to spend the night in the infirmary.

Naturally, I wasn't happy about it. It was draughty, creepy, and anyone who walked by looked at me like I was a drain on society. It wasn't any better than the barracks, so I wasn't sure what I was complaining about.

After showering, I slid into bed and stared at the comings and goings outside the clear plastic window. I didn't know how Elijah expected me to find a cure for something I didn't understand, all while keeping it from everyone in Camelot.

"Hey."

I looked up at the sound of Trent's voice. "Hey..." He moved and sat on the end of the bed. "I've got something for you."

"Should I be worried?"

"Not in the slightest." He reached inside his jacket and took out my arondight blade.

"You found it?" I snatched the hilt from his grasp and held it against my chest, the cool metal comforting. "I thought it was gone for good."

"I went back and looked for it," he explained. "I know how much it means to you."

He was right. Arondight blades were a personal thing. When we'd graduated from the Academy, we were all given the opportunity to choose our own hilts, though most of the time they chose us. Some were new, some were family heirlooms, and some were the weapons of fallen Naturals. The heirlooms chose by blood of course, but for those who didn't have that link, sometimes the blade they ended up with was a surprise.

My sword had been in the armoury for a long time. Several generations had gone by and no one had taken it up…until I'd walked in. Elizabeth Clare had been a decorated, yet troubled, warrior in the mid-eighteenth century. Stationed in Paris during the revolution, she'd seen some gruesome battles and had famously gone undercover with a demonic cult to root out a greater demon. It seemed fitting that her blade had chosen me.

"Do you want to talk about it?" Trent asked, breaking through my daydream.

I shook my head. "There isn't anything to talk about."

"They captured you."

I stared at him. "And?"

"And are you dealing with all of it?" he asked. "I know you're a private person, Mads, but even you have to admit that being tortured by a Balan demon had to suck."

"He didn't get very far," I murmured, remembering being kicked unconscious. Strange how these things had slipped my mind. I was oddly detached from it all. "He only got into my head once. I escaped before he could try again."

"What…what did you see?"

"The time Kayla used her Light to burn up my cheeks in the girls' bathrooms."

Trent hissed, "Shite. She did that?"

I shrugged. "It wasn't bad. Just a few burns that healed straight away."

"I didn't realise how badly they bullied you…"

"Don't get cut up about it, Trent," I told him. "That was a long time ago. Besides, we all made up, remember?"

"It doesn't—"

"Just stop," I snapped, my inner demon flaring. "I just want to leave that shite in the past, okay?" I flinched as soon as the words left my lips. I noticed the Dark edge to my psyche more and more. Whatever those creatures had blasted me with on the hillside must have triggered the thing back to life.

Trent scowled at me and stood. "Whatever, Madeleine. I was just trying to help, but like always, you're too stubborn to accept a simple gesture of kindness without it turning into a shite show."

He took two furious steps across the infirmary before I called out, "Trent?"

He turned, bracing for the impact of whatever barb he thought I was going to throw at him.

"I'm sorry. You're only trying to help me and…" Heat filled my cheeks. I didn't even know how to apologise properly.

"It's fine," he said with a sigh. "I'm just glad you're okay."

Unbidden tears prickled my eyes and I smiled. "Thanks."

His expression softened and he nodded. "Get some rest, okay?"

"Sure."

I watched him leave then sank back against the pillows and bit my lip to stifle a frustrated groan.

I had to control this thing before it ruined my life.

9
————

I twisted through the air, my staff following my movements.

The yard was empty, surrounded by low walls, and I was thankful for the solitude. It was a large space—around twenty by twenty metres with a sheltered alcove at one end—which made it perfect for its new inhabitants. What it used to be was a mystery, but it was now repurposed as a training space for the security team.

I escaped the infirmary as soon as I woke. Sharpening my skills was my happy place and right now, I needed all the happy I could get.

The staff was tipped with cold iron on both ends and counter weighed by a light stainless-steel haft. Smack a demon in the face with one of these, and the cold iron would burn its flesh. Not as effective as an arondight blade but handy, nonetheless.

I slammed the tip against the rubber training dummy in the chest, then turned and rapped the haft against its side. It vibrated back and forth under my assault, remaining annoyingly intact.

You're so worried about the things that you can't do, you're blind to the things you can.

Elijah's words echoed in my mind and my Light began to simmer. My arondight blade was heavy against my hip, a reminder of everything I'd worked for.

Naturals had relied on their swords to vanquish demons for almost a thousand years, but what if we didn't need them? Maybe with focused training, we could develop our powers into something more. Maybe…

I called on my Light, shaping it as it grew, and pushed it into the staff. I struck the dummy, testing the limits of the energised weapon, but all it did was snap and pop against the ballistics rubber like it was a pathetic little bug zapper.

I was blind to the things I could do? I didn't understand what Elijah meant.

I tried again, this time giving the staff a little more juice. Spinning, I arced the weapon around and slammed it into the dummy. The staff crackled and spluttered, and the little ball of demon inside me gurgled in response, almost like it was laughing at me.

Arsehole.

"What are you doing?"

I turned, closing my fist around my Light. Maisy stood a few paces away, watching me with a frown.

"Practising," I replied as I set the staff against the wall.

She tucked her chestnut hair behind her ear. "How are you?"

"Fine."

"Are you sure? I mean…" she stepped closer and lowered her voice, "the Dark captured you, Madeleine."

"Maisy, they trained us to deal with those kinds of situations." I looked her over and she flushed, more worried about it than I was—and I'd been the one locked in a cage. "Trent told you, didn't he?"

"Don't be mad at him, Madeline," she replied. "He's only trying to help."

By telling her they tortured me with images of the bullying she'd been a part of? What part of 'leave it in the past' didn't they understand?

Feeling a twist of anger rise inside me, I stilled and took a deep breath. "I wish you wouldn't."

"So you'd rather push everyone away and be alone than work through the things that are hurting you?"

I sighed, wondering what I'd done to get all the attention. "You're not helping by dragging up the past. Do you think I want to be reminded of all the horrible things I went through? There's working through stuff, and then there's constant torture."

"Madeleine—"

"*Just stop*," I hissed. "If you've got something to say to me to ease your guilt, then just say it. Don't make it your mission to fix my life—which is just fine, by the way—to make yourself feel better. It doesn't work that way, Maisy."

"I'm sorry," she blurted. "I'm real sorry, okay?"

"Do you feel better?"

"A little."

She stared at me, so I narrowed my eyes. "Anything else?"

"Thompson said you're excused from patrol tonight."

I shook my head. "You should have led with that."

"Are we good, I mean—"

"Of course, we are," I told her. "I know you're only trying to help, but you're just pressing the wrong buttons. I deal with things differently, that's all."

How did I reconcile the fact that my mutation might be the source of all my issues? It was a cruel joke to say the least.

Whatever this mutation was inside me, Ramona hadn't detected it. No one had, even after it had been activated by those slimy ex-Camelot demons. I wondered what it meant. Was it just a natural evolution . . . or was it something more sinister?

If it was active, would it grow? If it messed with my Light, I'd have a serious problem on my hands— one I wasn't sure I'd be able to keep secret for long.

My problem was I had too many questions and not enough answers.

"I just...I want to look to the future and do something I'd be proud of," I confided. "I don't want my past to be the only thing I'm remembered for."

Maybe Maisy could understand where I was coming from, being on her own redemption arc and everything.

She looked at the staff in my hands and then at the training dummy. "Do you want some company?"

I didn't, but in the interest of rebelling against the status quo—the status quo being my internal friend—I nodded. "Sure. I won't go easy on you, though."

She smiled, the uneasiness of our earlier conversation forgotten. "I wouldn't expect anything less."

<hr>

"We have to cut it out of her."

My eyes cracked open and fluttered as they filled with bright, white light.

"We can't, Ramona," someone said. "It could kill her."

"There's no other way."

I jerked my arms but was met with resistance.

"She's waking up." *Scarlett?*

"We're out of time," Ramona exclaimed. "We have to do it now."

"No!" The sounds of a scuffle reverberated around me and I fought against the restraints. "I won't let you take her!"

My limbs felt heavy like they had sedated me. I was having trouble opening my eyes and confusion filled my mind.

"Wait! Stop, I can explain…" I shouted, but my lips weren't moving. "Scarlett! Help me!"

Ramona's face came into view above me. "Don't worry, Madeleine. I'll cut the demon out of you."

Stop… *No*… Don't do this… Scarlett…

Elijah, *please…Elijah!*

"Madeline."

My eyes flew open and I reached for my cold iron dagger. Trent's hand wrapped around my wrist and I gasped for air. "What…?"

"You were screaming in your sleep," he said as the barracks came into focus behind him.

It seemed I'd woken everyone because they were standing around their beds, starting at me—annoyance, concern, anger…it was all there.

Trent noticed the direction of my gaze and waved at them. "It's okay, everyone," he said, "it's just the after-effects of her capture."

I shot him a withering glare and began to get dressed, wiping at the sweat across my brow. Shoving my feet into my trousers, I stood and pulled them up. I felt dizzy but nothing I couldn't dampen with Light.

"What are you doing?" he asked. "It's two in the morning."

"I can't stand it in here," I hissed as I grabbed my jacket. "Did you see their faces when you said the word capture? It sounded more like *collusion* to them."

He wrapped his hand around my arm. "Madeleine…"

I lowered my gaze, unsettled by my dream. "I just need to be alone for a while."

"You can't go outside the boundary."

I rolled my eyes and snatched my arondight blade. "I'll be fine." I had a guardian demon after all.

Outside, the camp was still. The low hum of the

generators echoed off the stone walls, but nothing else stirred—apart from the bleeding effect of my hallucination.

It'd been so real. Ramona had warned me, but I'd brushed it off. I could handle anything my mind threw at me—except maybe undergoing a live autopsy.

I moved through the camp, the cool air soothing my flushed brow. The ground had turned into hard packed dirt from the hundreds of pairs of boots that had walked over it and I loathed to think what this place looked like after rain.

Finally, I slipped past the watch on the walls, keeping to the shadows. It was easier than I had expected, but they were looking for things trying to get in, not out.

I could breathe easier once I was outside the limits of Camelot. Climbing the hill, I kept an eye out for the patrols, but I'd seemed to have timed my wake-up call perfectly. I was alone…with about a trillion stars watching over me.

I found a sheltered alcove in a rocky outcrop near the top of the rise and turned towards the valley. Celestial beings, demons from a parallel universe, humans turned supernatural, hidden worlds and ancient wars . . .. Our world was a strange one, that was for sure.

Despite the bright moonlight, Camelot was a dark smudge on the landscape. I never cared what lay within the depths of the castle, but I wondered what it was like when it was intact and full of life. This was the pinnacle of our civilisation—if you could call it that—until everything had gone wrong. The fickle human heart had almost destroyed the entire world. Speaking of fickle…

What was I going to do about Elijah? There was no cure for his mutation. Not one that I could see at least. Ramona had only stopped mine because it hadn't completely taken over. Elijah's had deep roots that'd likely fused with his humanity over the years.

How could anyone be cured of something so parasitic and not die? I didn't think it was possible. It'd only been one day, but Ramona had already given me the answer to his predicament. There was nothing I could do for him unless he wanted to come back to Camelot, but I knew he'd refuse.

Looked like it was bad news for me. Would Elijah let me live now that I knew about him?

"Back so soon?"

I spun on my heel, my heart leaping into my throat as Elijah melted out of the darkness.

"Don't do that!" I hissed, keeping my voice low. Sound carried out here and the last thing I needed was to bump into a patrol.

"You're the one who called me."

"No, I didn't…" I frowned, trying to recall the moment when I had summoned him, but came up empty.

"You did. But it seems like you didn't mean to." He turned to walk away, but something made me grab his arm.

"Elijah."

He glanced at my hand, then back over his

shoulder at me. Heat swam into my cheeks and I let him go, turning back towards Camelot.

I sat on the ledge and propped my feet up onto a rock. "It's harder than I thought."

A ripple passed through my body as Elijah arranged himself next to me, our boots pressing against each other. I noted he was careful not to touch me anywhere that risked skin on skin contact, but at least he was sticking around.

"Whatever those demons did to me, it woke up my residual mutation," I said. "I'm aware of it now."

"So, in simple terms, it means you're more of a raging bitch than usual?"

I snorted and wrapped my arms around my knees. "If I didn't have this stupid thing inside me, I would be well-adjusted. Wouldn't that be a novelty?"

Maybe I was asking myself the wrong questions. It should be more like *how* to get rid of it, rather than *why* it was there.

We fell into a strange silence, the whispers carried on the wind our only company.

After a moment, Elijah stirred. "Why are you here?"

"I couldn't sleep. The…" I trailed off, not wanting to share my weakness with him.

"Ah," he murmured, "the echoes. They'll pass."

I relaxed a little, knowing I had the human side of him with me. While he was amicable, I wondered if he'd reveal more about who he was, then maybe I wouldn't feel so stupid about wanting to spend time with him—which was a betrayal to the Naturals.

I studied his profile. "How old are you exactly?"

"Twenty-eight human years," he replied matter-of-factly.

"I don't believe you," I scoffed.

He smirked, his eyes shimmering silver in the moonlight. "If you want the answers you seek, then you have to ask the right questions."

Fine. "How long have you been twenty-eight?"

"A lot longer than I should have."

"Now you're deliberately evading the question."

His lips quirked and he turned to look at Camelot. I had to tell him the truth—and the perfect time was now, while his demon side was asleep.

"Elijah…they never finished their research," I told him. "There's nothing I can give you."

His shoulders tensed.

"It'll take time and I'm not sure—"

"I've got plenty of time," he interrupted, jerking on the tether that bound us. "*Keep trying*. Your cure could be mine."

I grimaced as a strange pressure wrapped around my chest and squeezed. I imagined it was what a heart attack felt like.

"You don't have to hurt me," I hissed and jerked away from him. "I would have helped you without all this binding shite."

"You forget what I am." His tone had turned cold. His demon half had roused.

"I forget *nothing*."

We were nose-to-nose, within an inch of

something more intimate, yet we held steady. I was lost and he was…unknown.

Elijah lowered his gaze before returning it to mine. "You close yourself off from others, yet you give everything to me—*the enemy*—without a second thought. Why is that?"

I tensed, knowing I was playing with fire, but unable to stop myself. When I was with him, my pain went away.

"I don't know," I murmured. "Maybe I am just a stupid little girl after all."

10

———

I stood my ground as Thompson glared at me.

The security tent was empty, but the sounds of base camp filtered through the thick canvas.

"Leaving camp boundaries without permission is a punishable offence," he barked. "And after your ordeal, it baffles me as to why you'd even want to."

I didn't reply, though holding my tongue had become difficult.

"I don't know what to do with you, Madeline," he said with an exasperated sigh. "You and I both know that this is your last chance. I don't want to report you to the Regula, but you're leaving me no choice. Haven't you got anything to say for yourself?"

The tent flap opened and Aiden strode in, followed by a gust of cool air. *Saved by the younger brother.*

He looked at his brother, then at me. "I can't say I'm surprised, but I spoke to Trent this morning. He said you woke up the entire barracks because of an echo."

I lowered my gaze, but not before catching Thompson's glare.

"Why didn't you say?" he demanded.

"Would it have changed your response?" I asked him.

"There's no need to report anything here." Aiden stepped between us before Thompson could reply. "I think you'd benefit from helping us on the dig, Madeline. We are always in need extra hands."

I raised my eyebrows. First it was a demotion to running patrols, now it was down to digging through piles of dirt?

"There's increased demon activity around the perimeter," I argued.

"I informed the Regula of your findings," Thompson said, "and they're launching an investigation."

My eyes widened. "You spoke to Wilder?"

"The Inquisitor ordered the scouting of Ben Nevis himself," he told me.

But they didn't need me. Wilder hadn't checked in either, which was another blow I hadn't expected.

"Given the circumstances, they've sent more experienced Naturals," Aiden said. "We'd rather have you here, Madeline. You've been back for three days and Ramona was adamant about the echoes lasting for a week or more."

"We have removed you from active duty until further notice," Thompson stated.

"I feel fine," I said. "I can't be benched again. I—"

"You're not losing your status," Aiden said. "You'll be able to return to duty when you're medically cleared."

"That's an order."

I glanced at Thompson and nodded. "Understood."

"Dismissed." He waved at his brother as if to say *good luck with that*. "Aiden, she's all yours."

Outside, Aiden gestured for me to follow him and he led me though base camp towards Camelot. Another new assignment…

I glowered, annoyed I wasn't going to be part of the investigation of Ben Nevis, though I supposed my report had been enough. Elijah wouldn't have been happy about me leaving Camelot anyway.

"This isn't a punishment, Madeleine," Aiden explained. "This might be good for you."

Digging up broken and crusty pottery out of the ground would be good for me? What planet was he on?

"I could help Ramona in the infirmary," I offered, seeing a chance to get myself unbound from a certain demon-hybrid. "I don't know anything about archeology."

"It's easy when you know the basics," he countered. "Besides, the infirmary doesn't see much action. You'd just be sitting around all day."

I narrowed my eyes. There was plenty to do in the infirmary, but I couldn't tell him that.

"Try it," Aiden told me. "At least until the echoes subside."

"Aren't you afraid I'll break something?"

"Not at all. I'll get you started on some basic stuff."

"*Great.*"

"I have the perfect place you can start," he said, ignoring my veiled sarcasm. "Follow me."

I cleared my mind as we walked, thinking over my situation.

If I was going to have any chance of helping Elijah, I had to make good with everyone. Win some trust, then work my way into the infirmary and science labs and learn some basics so I could diagnose myself—all while trying to subdue my temperamental parasite.

I knew some simple things about my original mutation from when I was sick, but I hadn't paid a lot of attention. Those early days after Scarlett had saved my soul were a blur. Then I had to deal with the loss of my Light—the very thing that made me a Natural.

Basically, I was starting from scratch.

We passed through the limits of the outer city, decaying towers and parapets looming in the distance. This place must have been a marvel to look at, but now it was a shell crawling with excited archaeologists with little shovels.

Even from this distance, I could see part of the castle was carved out of the cliff face, and the rest of the structure flowed down into the lower valley in formidable steps. I'd looked out over the city a few times now, but the lay of the land and the illusions hiding it from human eyes had concealed Camelot's true size. Now that I could see it, I began to understand why everyone was so fascinated by its mysteries. There were so many hidden corners.

"Impressive, isn't it?" Aiden commented. "They must have used so much Light to conceal it. It's like it exists in its own pocket of space beyond the outside world."

"Maybe the Druids and the Lady of the Lake helped make this place like Avalon…hidden in time."

"Perhaps. Though I wonder if it's more likely there's a power source."

I raised my eyebrows, never hearing about such a thing. "Like a battery?"

"Who knows for sure? Whatever it is, it's still active." Aiden shrugged. "Camelot is full of beauty and mystery. We've found everything from simple spoons, all the way to jewellery, elaborate mosaics, and painted murals. There are even some artefacts that have carried faint traces of Light."

I'd overheard some Naturals talk about the mosaic courtyard outside the main gates of the castle. Only a few had seen it, as it led to the ruined chasm opened by Arthur and Lancelot when they'd crossed their swords, Excalibur and Arondight.

The entrance was set with intricate mosaic scenes of battles, knights on horseback, Druidic runes, the Pendragon crest, and the Lady of the Lake—or so I'd heard.

"Do you think there's anything demonic left?" I asked.

"Not that we've found, but there is the possibility."

Aiden turned a corner, leading me down a narrow street. "It's possible the Darkness was chased out when the Twin Flames closed the rift, but we can't be too careful. We have protocols and failsafes in place to catch any traps that may have been left behind."

That was reassuring. I looked around at the street Aiden had led me down. The lower city pressed closer here. They had erected buildings in every available space, some with two and even three stories. How many Naturals had lived here? More than I could imagine…and they'd all been taken in the cataclysm. It was a bitter pill to swallow, but at least the war was over.

For now.

I swallowed hard as my mutation stirred. It felt like stomach acid and the metaphor wasn't lost on me. I should own up to it, but—

"Here we are," Aiden declared. "Come and look."

I studied the building with an underwhelmed sigh. It sat on an open square surrounded by stone structures just like it. There was even a fountain in the middle with a statue that had crumbled away at the knees.

"What is it?" I asked as I followed Aiden inside.

It must have been a house or a hall at some point, but the roof was long gone. There was the triangular stone remains of the structure at both ends, and a large fireplace with its mantle missing. Like everything else around here, anything organic had rotted away.

The stonework of the outer wall was intricate considering it was merely simple blocks. Each cut was so precise, there was no need for mortar to hold it all together. There were even some strange angles that made the façade look like a puzzle—Medieval zero waste—and I doubted I'd be able to slip a piece of paper between the cracks.

Before us, they had set the earthen floor out in a large grid with a string wrapped around each peg, dividing the space with a dozen two-metre square sections. That's as far as work had progressed here. No one had dug here yet and it seemed like I had the honour of breaking ground.

At least it was quiet and I'd be alone. The last thing I wanted was to break some priceless artefact and have an audience to witness it. My constant run of unfortunate incidents was bad enough.

"We think it was an inn or a tavern," Aiden replied, answering my earlier question.

He knelt inside a square and motioned for me to join him. Not worrying about dirtying my clean trousers, I knelt beside him.

"What do I do?"

He placed his palms on the sectioned-off earth. "Let me show you."

I pressed my hands next to his, the grit digging into my skin. "Now what?"

"Use your Light to sense what's underneath the ground." I felt the dirt ripple as he sent a pulse outwards. "Just a little."

"Like a radar detector," I mused.

"It takes some practice, but you can learn to tell apart different materials—stone, copper, clay, iron, gold—and their estimated shapes." He nodded towards the ground. "Have a go."

I took a deep breath, forgetting how silly I must look, and closed my eyes. My palms warmed, then I sent a gentle wave of Light into the ground. As my power flowed through me, I could feel its journey as it filtered through the layers of dirt. Almost immediately, it seemed to bump against something, then kept going.

I opened my eyes. "I think there's something here."

"Let's dig then." Aiden smiled and handed me a trowel. "You want to go slow to avoid damaging any artefact that may be buried. Scrape away the surface soil, then chip down in small scoops."

I grasped the trowel and began to scrape off the hardened surface layer. Once I'd cleared it, I began to edge deeper. My heart beat faster as I wondered what I might unearth.

Then the edge of my trowel hit something solid.

"I've found something." Excitement filled my heart and I dug around the object, revealing the smooth surface of a glazed pot. "What is it?"

"It's a cup," Aiden replied simply as I uncovered more of the object. "Wow, would you look at that?"

I took a little brush from him and dusted over the exposed ceramic, revealing the design painted and pressed into the fired clay. Three yellow crowns inside a blue shield—the Pendragon coat of arms. It was a simple cup, but it was from the time of Arthur and the cataclysm. Someone had held this almost a thousand years ago, maybe even on the night the rift opened.

Aiden chuckled and sat back on his heels. "Now do you get it?"

I looked up at him and nodded. "I'm sorry I called you a bunch of nerds."

His chuckle turned into a full belly laugh. "Welcome to the fold, honorary nerd."

<hr>

After a few days working on the dig, things were getting better.

I was careful not to go to Aiden with every little question to avoid the jealous women who had crushes on him. Instead, I asked the other archeologists how to do things and shared what I found—I'd since added some silver coins to my cup. I showed interest in their work and said nothing personal and soon, I'd become just another face in the Camelot dig.

Two other Naturals joined me the day after I'd begun work inside the inn. Carly from the Los Angeles Sanctum and Heath from the Edinburgh outpost. They were cordial enough towards me, but not openly hostile, so we worked in amicable silence for most of the day.

What surprised me the most was how I was treated outside of the security detail. There was less hostility in the air, and I could breathe for the first time since I was a teenager.

Unearthing the hall was slow going. Now I'd

learned the intricacies of the job, I understood why so little of Camelot was uncovered. Too heavy a hand and something of great importance and value could be accidentally destroyed.

"Hey!" A woman leaned though the doorway and waved to the others. "They've found something up at the castle. Everyone's going to check it out."

She vanished as soon as she appeared, and I glanced at Carly and Heath. They began to chatter excitedly, then stepped out of their squares.

I hesitated. My settings were still on isolation mode and I wondered if I should go, too.

As if she'd read my thoughts, Carly paused at the door and turned back. "*Madeleine*," she said with a good-humoured sigh, "are you coming or not?"

I grinned and dropped my trowel. "For sure."

Excited to be included—even in a small way—I followed them through the lower city. Soon I was turning into a large thoroughfare that led up to the inner castle of Camelot. It was a new section I hadn't been to before—a more posh part by the looks of it. I tried to remember some things Aiden had taught us in history class back at the Academy. How the poorer people lived on the outer edges, then the higher ranked and their sacks of gold, followed by the nobility, and then the kings and queens. It was a theme that still presented itself in modern cities all around the world.

I followed the other Naturals up a flight of stairs and almost crashed into a crowd of fifty or so people at the top. Cursing, I edged around them, standing on my tiptoes to see what they were looking at.

"Can you believe it?" someone said. "Hidden right beneath our feet this whole time!"

"I know, right?" a woman replied. "Can you imagine what else is hidden here?"

Finally, I found a gap between the excited archaeologists. There was a huge hole in the middle of another square that sat against the immense outer wall of Camelot's inner castle.

Aiden and his team had partially dug out a freestanding building that appeared to have sunk into the earth hundreds of years ago. It sat well below the original paving as if someone had hidden it—by what or who, it was impossible to tell. The walls were plastered and painted, though the colours had faded and the stone underneath showed through.

From what I could make out, the design was Druidic. Runes were woven in reliefs depicting a woman in a flowing gown with stars in her hair. Was it the Lady of the Lake? It was difficult to tell with so much of the structure still buried.

"I heard Aiden say it looked like it was intentionally buried."

My ears pricked up. I turned so I could listen to the archeologists' gossip.

"There's power in the ground here, can't you feel it?"

"It's a chamber," the woman in front of me said. "This part of the city was fortified, which means it was important. We're inside the walls of the inner castle, you know."

"What do you think it is?" the man asked. "A treasury?"

"Maybe. It seems untouched by the Dark. Can you believe it?"

Nausea rippled through my body and I leaned against the stone wall. Why did I feel so sick? My Light should… It was then that I realised it was my mutation reacting to something.

I glanced around, but no one was looking at me. They were all excited about the strange building buried underneath the city. But the longer I looked at it, the more I knew it should probably be left alone.

Who knew what secrets the Naturals had buried under here, let alone what the Dark had twisted into the shadows? It was one thing to dig up a cup and some ancient coins, but quite another when it came to secret buildings.

Spotting Aiden by the wall, I tried to move forwards but the excited nerd brigade pushed me back.

I scowled and craned my neck so I could see deeper inside the hole. Maybe it was a good thing I couldn't get close.

The Dark had been after me from the beginning, but the creatures who'd taken me were from Camelot. What if they were looking for something they'd left behind?

Suddenly, I had a sick feeling that the Balan demon had planned to turn me into a double agent

and retrieve it for him. I wasn't sure which was the
most moronic thing I was keeping a secret about—
Elijah or my lingering mutation.

Oh man, this was getting worse by the minute.

Edging away from the excitement, I dragged
myself thought the lower city and back to my square.
I'd just have to hope I was smart enough to keep one
step ahead of the Dark.

11

Music ebbed through the Camelot base camp, the modern sounds of rock and pop jarring against the backdrop of the ruined castle.

Apparently, the discovery of a secret chamber warranted a party. I wasn't about to complain about the free beer, but times like these always reminded me of my outsider status amongst my own people.

I sat on an empty crate just outside the glow of the bonfire, nursing a bottle of beer brought up from the human village below. A group of Naturals from the security team had challenged each other to do backflips over the flames, and I watched them with a heavy heart. Maybe I'd be with them right now if I hadn't been infected.

Depression sat heavy on my shoulders and I turned around, watching the comings and goings from another direction.

Man, I hated parties…but being ostracised was the least of my worries.

I knew I should say something to Aiden about the strange building, but I was stuck between a rock and a hard place. He'd want to know where my suspicions were coming from and I'd be forced to confess. Then everyone here with an axe to grind against the Dark—which was everyone after the losses from the Dark Night—would have an excuse to lock me up for good.

Maybe I'd be able to get some help, but the Regula wouldn't let me fight again—I'd broken the rules one too many times. If I was ousted, then I'd be leaving Elijah high and dry. If there was a chance to save him, then I should take it. I'd go down in flames either way, but at least he'd be free.

I sighed and sipped my beer. Too bad Naturals couldn't get drunk beyond tipsy.

"Hey, there you are."

I bristled as Maisy sat next to me, shoving me half off the crate.

"Hey, yourself."

"I'll bet you ten quid that someone lands arse first in the fire within the next half-hour."

I snorted and took another mouthful of beer.

Sensing my uneasiness, she knocked her shoulder against mine. "How's the dig?"

"Okay, I guess," I replied with a shrug. "It's slow going."

"Well, you're not missing much. Things have gone silent since…you know."

"You can say it, Maisy. I won't dissolve into tears."

She laughed and shook her head. "You're the toughest person I know, Madeleine. Of course not!"

I smiled. "It's good to hear. About the patrols, not the tears."

"I know, right? How's everything else? Any more echoes?"

I shook my head. "No. Whatever Ramona gave me to ease them seems to have worked."

"Oh good. That dream the other night sounded…"

I shivered. "Yeah, I know."

Maisy looked up at the sky and sighed. "Sometimes I wish I'd taken up another specialty."

"Huh?" I handed her my beer and she sipped absently. "You don't want to be a warrior?"

"How are we supposed to know what we want to do with our lives at seven?"

I frowned and began to wonder the same thing. "Well…"

"A duplicitous demon like her gets special treatment and all we get is patrol night after night."

I hesitated as the conversation behind us broke through our own. It wasn't like I didn't know people talked about me, but this was different. I had the overwhelming awareness they wanted me to hear. Kids could be cruel, but adults had the means to know better.

"Give her a break, Rhys," another man said. "She was captured—"

"*Exactly*," he interrupted. "Who knows what they did to her. For all we know, she staged it."

"C'mon," a woman scoffed, "I saw her when she

came back. She was definitely not a willing participant."

"You're so blind, Felicity," Rhys declared. "Demons lie. It's their nature."

I tensed, his words hit home. He was right. I was lying about everything, including the demon mutation that lingered inside me.

Maisy tugged on my sleeve. "Don't. He's not worth losing your position over. Let it go." She offered me my beer back as a distraction but I shook my head.

"She almost killed all those innocent kids at the Academy," Rhys went on. "She almost cost us Arondight! You know it's only a matter of time before she kills us all."

"Stop talking like that," the woman named Felicity hissed.

"Once a demon, *always a demon.*"

"She wouldn't be here if she was compromised," the man said.

"Zero tolerance." Rhys's volume increased and I knew he was making sure I heard every single word he said. I was well-versed in the art of a bully, after all. "We should send her back where she came from."

"Rhys, cut it out," Felicity said. "You don't mean that."

"Maybe he's right," the man muttered. "We won the war, but the Dark will do anything to stay alive."

"I say we throw her back," Rhys declared. The chatter of the party began to quiet as everyone turned to hear what was going on.

I lowered my gaze, my cheeks burned and my hands shook.

The sound of crunching boot steps echoed behind me, each one moving closer to where Maisy and I sat.

"Demon spawn should go back into the rift," Rhys continued. "All we need to do is pick her up and throw her into the chasm. It's only a matter of time before she turns Dark and kills us all. Once we're gone…" he clucked his tongue, "no one will be left to protect the world from being consumed. How does it feel, Madeleine? Huh? How does it feel knowing you will murder eight billion people?"

I rose to my feet. By this point someone had turned off the music and the entire camp was silent. It didn't mean much to me, we could've been on Mars for all I cared.

Turning, I struggled to keep hold of my rage. It wasn't my fault I'd been possessed and mutated as a teenager. I'd been a victim and ever since, my own people had shamed me for something out of my control, despite fighting tooth and nail to uphold Natural values and fight against the lingering Dark.

Rhys smirked as our gazes met. I barely knew the guy from a lump of coal, but he seemed to think he knew all about me.

"Throw her back!" he shouted to the others. "*Throw her back!*"

I fisted my hands into the front of his T-shirt and shoved him up against the wall. "*Say that again.*"

"*Madeline,*" Maisy hissed, tugging at my sleeve.

"Yeah, Madeleine," Rhys said with a sarcastic lit

in his voice, "you don't want to get thrown out of Camelot. This is your last chance, isn't it?"

"How can you sleep at night knowing how much of a worthless piece of shite you are?" I asked, gritting my teeth. "Does it make you feel better about your meaningless life to hate on others? You don't know the first thing about me."

"Like I said…" He leaned closer, his lips curving in a malicious grin. "Once a demon, always a demon."

A spark of uncontrollable anger burst to life inside me and I raised my fist and hit Rhys square in the nose. The sound of cracking bone was loud enough that the other Naturals gasped in shock, but it barely registered in my brain.

The mutation gurgled and spluttered its approval as blood began to pour from Rhys' nose.

"Say it again!" I shouted, but he didn't reply. "Not such a big man now, are you?"

He let out a strangled cry and lunged at me, slamming his shoulder into my chest. I stumbled backwards, ducking as his fist flew at my face.

"Beating up in a girl. *You're such a big man,*" I taunted him, smashing my shoulder into his ribs.

He hit the wall and caught my ankle with his boot. The blow sent me to my knees, then I was on my back rolling through the dirt as he landed on top of me.

We were a mess of fists and rage…and no one stopped us.

"Enough!" Like a spectre in the night, Thompson

appeared out of nowhere and pulled me off Rhys. "What's the meaning of this?"

I scrambled to my feet and wiped the back of my hand across my mouth. "Just teaching a prejudiced arsehole a lesson."

Rhys was on his feet in an instant. "You broke my nose!" He lunged at me, despite our commanding officer standing between us.

Thompson growled and shoved him backwards. "Stand down," he barked.

"You're nothing but a pathetic bully," I growled at my tormentor.

"*Greenbriar,*" Thompson snapped. He clicked his fingers at another Natural. "Take Rhys to the supply tent and await my arrival."

Rhys shoved off the hand that reached for him. "Sir—"

"*That's an order.*" I'd never seen Thompson so mad as he turned to face me. "And you will come with me."

I hissed as he grabbed my arm and dragged me away from the bonfire, the entire base camp staring in stunned silence.

Thompson's grasp hissed against my skin, the mutation sparking like it had the night the demons had captured me on patrol. I had to get a grip.

It wasn't long before Thompson shoved me into a tent at the opposite side of the camp—far away from the supply tent where Rhys had been taken.

I tensed as I felt Thompson's Light slam closed around me. They weren't the bars of the cage under

Ben Nevis, but they may as well have been. All that was missing was the meat closet.

"You better not be putting that trash in here with me," I drawled, turning on my heel. The limits of the tent were my boundary and breaking through the barrier was near impossible.

"You drew blood in an unprovoked attack." Thompson shook his head, his disappointment clear. "What were you thinking?"

"It was entirely provoked." I glared at him. "I think the words he used were, *'Throw her back'*." Thompson frowned at me, so I added, "Into the rift. That's where demon scum come from, you know."

"When someone baits you, you don't react," he exclaimed, throwing his hands into the air. "We're trying to help you, Madeleine, but you're not making it easy."

"You try to rise above when someone's trying to incite a lynch mob against you."

His lips thinned and he sighed. "*Light help me.*"

I knew it was the mutation bleeding into my emotions, but I was far too angry to push it back into its box.

"Sleep it off," Thompson said after a moment. "We'll discuss this in the morning when everyone has calmed down."

I narrowed my eyes. "Good luck with that."

"It's you who'll need luck." With one last glare, he strode from the tent, leaving me to stew in the fight's aftermath.

Cursing, I looked around, only to find a stainless-steel table and a few empty crates from the science division stacked against one side. It was going to be a long, cold night alone with the threat of being thrown out of Camelot in the morning, but that was the point.

They had thrown me in jail.

12

———

M*adeline.*

I sat bolt upright, almost hitting my head on the stainless-steel table. Confused, I rubbed my eyes.

I was still in the tent, locked in by Thompson's Light. It was dark outside, the party long over, but something had woken me.

It was another echo. I laid down on the hard ground with a sigh. Sleeping in a draughty tent full of trash—without a mattress or pillow—wasn't how I pictured my last hours at Camelot, but beggars couldn't be choosers.

I had to stand up for myself, right? Having a mutation push my emotions over the edge wasn't useful in the grand scheme of things, but I couldn't let Rhys get away with that kind of behaviour, either.

Oh, what the hell did it matter? I'd drawn blood one too many times and when the sun rose, they'd take my arondight blade and I would be exiled.

My eyes drooped as I lulled back into a restless sleep. Hope was a fickle thing when it came into contact with me.

Madeleine… Help…

My chest tightened and I gasped, my eyes flying open. That was so not a dream. Hissing, I rubbed the heel of my hand against my sternum. It felt as if something was tearing me open.

The bond. If this was Elijah's attempt at hurrying me up, he was in for a rude shock.

"Elijah, you better stop that or else." I scowled and doubled over. "I'm working on it, okay?"

Yeah, so that last bit was a lie. The finding a cure bit was a total bust now that I'd broken Rhys's nose. I guess I had another reckoning coming my way. Elijah could just take a number and get in line.

My vision blurred and for a split-second, I was lying on rocky ground—cold, weak, and alone. My chest burned as I dragged myself towards faint lights in the distance. *Camelot.*

I gasped as the tent came back into focus.

Elijah.

It took me a few minutes to get my bearings and once I did, I knew he was in serious shite. He hadn't used our link to punish me—he'd used it to call for help.

Standing, I walked over to the closed tent flap. Damn Thompson and damn Rhys for being a bigoted arsehole. I bashed my fist against the side of the tent, and it rippled as I struck the invisible barrier which kept me locked inside.

There was no way out of here, unless… A dangerous thought popped into my mind and my dormant mutation stirred. Dangerous wasn't the only word I thought of—intoxicating, deadly, and moronic. Even thinking about nullifying Thompson's Light with my theoretical Darkness was the most insane, reckless, and stupid thing I'd ever considered. That's if it even worked.

I shook my head and began to pace. Why was I even considering helping Elijah? He'd saved me twice —at *Adrenaline* and Ben Nevis—and he was…what? Handsome? *C'mon, Madeleine, stop being a stupid little girl and grow the hell up. This isn't a story about star-crossed lovers.*

Somewhere out in the hills, Elijah pulled on the tether and I almost threw up. Great, it seemed like I'd feel his death, and maybe even partake in it.

I sighed as I glanced at the tent flap. I was already facing a ninety-five percent chance of exile, so I might as well go for a perfect score.

Checking that my arondight blade was still at my hip, I thanked Thompson for his oversight and turned towards the flap. I unzipped it, opening the tent to the night.

Okay, think, Madeleine. Electricity flowed from negative to positive, which meant my mutation could affect my emotions by making my Light into a circuit. That was how I could access it and use it to negate Thompson's barrier and pass straight through. Theoretically, anyway.

All I had to do was complete the circuit between

my Light, my mutation, and the barrier, then I was out of here. I reached for the anger deep below my Light and hoped it would work.

Static charge began to crackle across my skin, twisting with a coldness that almost made me pull back. So this was what Darkness was like. I trembled, choking as my Light fought against it. *I couldn't lose control…* But thinking of Elijah, I let go.

I allowed the Darkness to fill me until I was unfeeling ice and charged rage. Pushing against the barrier, I grinned as my theory proved to be a raging success. *Those pathetic Naturals didn't stand a chance.*

I stepped through, Thompson's Light tugging at my hair, and then I was outside. Turning, I pressed my palm against the opening and snorted when I found the barrier still active. He'd be so mad when he showed up in the morning to find I'd vanished. The Dark part of me smirked, amused at the imminent chaos.

A tingling across my chest brought me back to the present and I slammed my Light closed around the mutation, cutting it off.

Holy shite…

Glancing around, I swallowed hard and began to move away from the tent, thankful that I was alone. If anyone had seen me do what I'd just done . . . . I'd be killed on the spot.

A skeleton crew was stationed throughout the camp and on the walls during the night, so it wasn't difficult to manoeuvre through the tent city unseen.

Unlike the London Sanctum, there weren't any alarms around Camelot my demonic friend could trigger, so there was zero fanfare when I passed the outer wall.

I'd just left everything I'd ever known behind, and I'd never be able to go back. My friends, my family, my entire reason for existing…*gone*. Moving away from Camelot, I knew there was no turning back now.

I stuck to the shadows, streaking across the landscape like a spectre. Patrols used the road in and out of the camp at regular intervals, and I had no idea what time it was and no time to wait. I took the risk and kept moving.

I darted away from the trail and up the hill, putting as much distance between me and Camelot as I could. Ducking below the rise, I cast my Light out, hoping I'd be able to sense Elijah just like I'd been able to sense those artefacts hidden underground.

Getting a hit farther into the rocky landscape, I clambered between boulders and scrambled over outcrops. This part of the Clee Hills was wild and untouched—it was on the outskirts of the illusion that hid Camelot, so humans hadn't been here in hundreds of years. The only thing that set foot in this part of the world were the Naturals and the Dark.

I set out another pulse, then turned left and leapt up onto a boulder. I shook my head as I scanned the shadowy maze. This was impossible. He should be right here.

"Elijah?" I called. "Answer me, damn you."

I jumped to the next boulder and skidded down the side. Looking over the edge of a shard of limestone, I found a natural alcove underneath. There, curled up in a tight ball, was Elijah.

He'd wedged himself between the rocks like a wounded animal, waiting for help or death, whichever came first.

"Elijah?"

The sound of my voice roused him and his head jerked towards me. Sensing his Darkness rising, I jumped down beside him and grasped his face.

"It's me," I murmured. "Madeleine."

That was when I realised he was covered in blood. It was smeared across his face and his T-shirt was tacky to the touch.

His power began to subside as his eyes focused on me. "Madeleine?"

"What happened to you?" I checked his pupils before I dragged his shirt up, looking for the source of the blood.

"Can't wait to get my clothes off, huh?" he rasped, swatting at my hands.

"Stay still." I shook my head and lifted the material away from his chest.

I swallowed my shock when I saw what the darkness was concealing. Three long gouges tore through his flesh, blood seeping from each one. It was difficult to tell how deep they were in the dark, but I didn't have to get out a ruler to understand how bad it was—or what had put them there.

"Elijah…"

"That bad, huh?" He coughed and grimaced as the movement pulled at his wounds.

"I have to get you back to Camelot."

"No," he rasped, "I can't go there."

"I can't leave you out in the open like this," I told him. "If a patrol finds you lying here, they'll drag you in for questioning. If I'm with you, at least they'll give you a chance."

He grabbed the lapels of my jacket and jerked me close. "I won't go there." His eyes flashed silver, his demonic side struggling against his humanity.

"Elijah, we don't have a choice."

"If I'm going to die, then I'm going to die free."

I hissed and helped him sit. "Why are men so stubborn?"

"I have a place," he told me, grasping at his chest.

I doubted his 'place' wasn't hospital-grade, but if he wouldn't let me take him back to base camp, then it was better than out in the open. "Is it safe?"

"I don't know."

"Well, I guess we'll find out." I sighed and threaded my arm underneath his and around his back. I heaved, using my Light to help get his bulk upright.

He grimaced and his knees buckled. If it wasn't for me, he would've collapsed, and I wasn't sure he'd be able to get back up.

"Did I call you?" he asked absently.

"Yeah," I replied, covering my concern, "you called me."

Elijah guided me away from Camelot to a part of the hills I hadn't seen before. Well outside the limits of Camelot's illusions, we found ourselves back in human territory.

It was slow going, but we staggered out of the hills and into a valley dotted with the beginnings of a forest.

We limped down a lane and around a bend before Elijah told me to stop by a copse of trees. "There."

I eased him against the stacked stone fence beside the lane. "I'm going to check inside."

He nodded, unable to help me even if he wanted.

Walking through the opening in the fence, I sent out a soft pulse of Light to scan my surroundings. The wave brushed up against some wards, and I stepped through to reveal Elijah's refuge.

It was an old crofter's cottage. The small, dark stone building had once belonged to a farmer who'd tended a field or two in centuries past. From the outside, it looked abandoned. Ivy tangled around the single chimney and one side of the house, giving it a haunted feel.

I walked up the uneven path. Nothing stirred other than the reverberations of the wards. Whatever he'd used to cloak this place, it wasn't Natural or demonic. It was a power I hadn't felt before and my suspicions began to grow.

The front door was unlocked. Easing it open, I stepped into the shadows.

To my surprise, the cottage was rather modern inside. Someone had updated the interior to include a simple kitchenette with a refrigerator and a functioning bathroom. The bed was in the living area as there wasn't a separate bedroom anywhere.

I ran my fingers over an empty shelf and frowned. There was nothing here that could give me a glimpse at Elijah's true identity. Every wall and surface were bare of personal effects. If he had a home, this certainly wasn't it.

I returned to Elijah once I was satisfied there was no threat waiting for us.

"It hasn't been touched," I told him. "Let's get you inside."

We made it up the uneven path and into the cottage, hidden away from the outside world. For the moment, we were safe from both the Light and the Dark.

I helped Elijah onto the bed and eased his jacket off his shoulders. His face contorted in pain, but he didn't make a sound. Next came his T-shirt.

There was a stack of candles on the bedside table that had dripped wax all over the place. I lit them with my Light, and a little warmth fell over the bed.

In the flickering candlelight, I could see his wounds. Three deep rents had opened him up from one side to the other, exposing muscle underneath. Nothing vital seemed to be punctured, but he'd lost a great deal of blood. He might be half-demon with his own brand of Darkness, but it wouldn't save his human body from infection.

I wondered how he'd stood, let alone made it all the way here without blacking out. If I didn't know he was half-demon, I'd be wondering why he wasn't dead already.

"Don't give me that look," he muttered, his gaze on the floor.

"Lie back, okay? I'm going to clean you up."

I found some washcloths in the bathroom and a bowl in the kitchen. I filled the latter with water and returned to Elijah's bedside. Soaking the cloth, I wrung it out and began to clear the blood from his chest.

Once I could see what I was doing, I began to manipulate my Light around the torn flesh. It must have been painful, but he didn't move, his eyes open and blank. If it wasn't for his fingers twisting around the blanket, I would've thought he was gone.

As his body began to respond to my attempts at first aide, I sighed. The bleeding began to ease, and some wounds began to close. There was no way I could heal him completely—that was an ability reserved for the Twin Flames.

Elijah needed proper medical attention with surgical instruments and medicine, not a musty cottage and a Natural who only knew basic flesh manipulation.

"You've got blood on you."

I met Elijah's gaze and grunted. "It's yours. You're torn apart, if you haven't noticed."

"It's not all mine."

"Oh, I..." I glanced down at my T-shirt and rubbed my palm across the stain. I wasn't sure if it was mine or Rhys's blood. "How can you tell?"

"Demons have a knack for all things blood," he replied.

Right. That wasn't creepy at all. "Yeah, uh...I got into a fight."

"About?"

I made a face and sat beside him. "You want to know right now?"

"Humour me." He wanted a distraction. Couldn't blame him, considering.

"This guy... He accused me of being a demon."

Elijah snorted. "Technically, he's right."

I screwed up my face. "Do you want me to leave you here?" I made to stand, but he grasped my wrist, despite the pain moving must have caused him.

"*No.*"

My heart leapt and I swallowed hard. "I won't go."

Relief flashed through his eyes and he sank back against the pillows.

"What happened to you?" I murmured.

"They tried to kill me," he whispered, his eyes fluttering closed. "The Balan..."

"He found out you helped me escape, didn't he?"

Elijah nodded and I curled my hands into fists. I knew what this meant. He'd been working with the Balan all this time. I began to regret breaking out of Camelot to save him.

"You were working with him all this time, weren't you?" I asked.

"It's not what it looks like…"

"Then it means you're playing both sides."

"It isn't so bad," he said with a smirk.

"Someone with split allegiances isn't to be trusted. One minute they're your friend, the next, they're putting a knife in your back if it gets them what they want."

He scowled and turned his head.

"You have to give me something, Elijah. I just threw away my entire life to save you. It can't have been all for nothing."

His expression faded and he returned his gaze to mine. "What?"

"Camelot was my last chance," I hissed. "And I just blew everything. The Dark captured me, I started a fight that got me locked up, and I just broke out against the direct orders of my superior officer…and I used my mutation to do it! Your chance at finding a cure just went up in smoke and I betrayed my people."

His hand found mine. "Madeleine…"

"I can't help you." I shook my head. "I can't even help myself. If you want your cure, I have to take you to Camelot and beg Ramona to help you. It's that simple."

"But if you go back—"

"I'll be stripped of my arondight blade and charged with consorting with the enemy. I'll be thrown into the prison under Glastonbury and left to rot."

He sighed, his brow creasing. "I'll take my chances out here."

"It's not just your cure," I said, my grip tightening on his hand. "Your wounds——"

"Will heal or they won't," he snapped.

"Do you want to die that much?" I swallowed my frustrated tears before they betrayed how deep I was in this strange relationship.

The question seemed to be one step too far for Elijah and he remained tight-lipped.

What was I going to do? I'd lost everything the moment I'd left that tent. Dangerous as it was, Elijah was the only person I had left, and I wasn't even sure I could trust him.

"Whose side are you really on?" I asked.

"*Mine.*"

I sighed. It was harder to get answers out of him than blood out of a stone.

"You do know that every time you think about me, I feel a little tug."

I groaned. "That doesn't sound dirty *at all.*"

He coughed, his brow creasing as he held onto his pain. "Admit it. You've got the hots for me."

"*In your dreams.* You bound me to you, remember?" I hesitated. "What will happen to me if…"

"Nothing," he told me. "If I die, you'll be free."

I didn't understand. He was lying there, vulnerable, and he'd just told me how to free myself from his tether. There was nothing stopping me from taking his life and leaving him here to rot.

"Why would you tell me that?" I demanded.

He grasped my wrist and pulled me close. "There are shades of grey in this world, Madeleine. It's not all Darkness." My breath caught. "They took my colours, you know."

I didn't have any idea what he was talking about. Pressing my palm against his forehead, I felt the heat radiate off him. Not only were his wounds not healing, they were showing signs of infection. That meant I wasn't going to get many coherent answers tonight.

"Shh," I murmured, "you need your rest."

"You could free yourself right now," he raved. "I wouldn't blame you if you did. Go into hiding and save yourself. *Go*."

"I'm not going anywhere." I wet another washcloth and dabbed it against his forehead. "Despite my better judgement, you're stuck with me."

He studied me for a long time. When it was getting unbearable, he said, "The Balan wants something in Camelot."

"I already know that."

"I think he's using us to get to it. If you take me there…"

"The world will not implode if we go to Camelot, Elijah. It will suck for us, but the Earth will continue to spin."

"*It won't…*" he whispered. "Lately, I feel *drawn* there."

Dread began to rise inside me. The mysterious room Aiden uncovered…

"One last chance," I said, taking his hands in mine. "Whose side are you on, Elijah?"

His gaze met mine, and for the first time it was clear. "Yours," he said. "I want to be on yours."

13

The long fingers of dawn stretched across the cottage and filtered through the window.

I jerked awake, my eyes gritty with sleep. The armchair was hard against my back, the awkward position tensed up my muscles. Combing my fingers through my hair, I peered outside, my nerves on edge.

My predicament hadn't sunk all the way in yet, and the harsh light of a new day laid everything bare.

Betrayal. Darkness. Hate. Loneliness.

I hadn't thought twice about leaving or giving in to the Darkness hiding within. I'd lived up to all the years of rumours and gossip, and it was a bitter pill to swallow.

Who was I without my arondight blade? I still had it, but I'd never weld it against the Dark in the same way ever again.

Madeleine Greenbriar had died last night, and a stranger was born in her place.

I rubbed my eyes and rose, shoving away the unwelcome thoughts. Me spiralling into depression was the last thing we needed right now.

I sat beside Elijah on the bed, careful not to disturb his sleep. His wounds had scabbed over, but they were still red and angry, and heat radiated off him like a furnace. Frowning, I replaced the washcloth with a new one, hoping to ease even a small amount of his fever.

The coolness stirred him and his eyes opened.

"Sorry, I didn't mean to wake you," I murmured, dabbing his brow. The old Madeleine would've shied away from the intimate touch, but the new one didn't break stride.

"Why did you come for me?" he whispered, half asleep.

"I guess you're the last person alive that's like me. You understand."

"Liar."

I laid the cloth across his forehead and scoffed, "Isn't that your speciality?"

"You're like me, remember?"

"Smart arse."

He chuckled softly.

"I understand now. Well, at least a little." I lowered my gaze. "When I tapped into my mutation, it was like…"

"You were another person?"

I lifted my head. "Yeah. I was all…cold, ruthless. The chaos…t excited me."

"You're lucky," he said. "Your Light contains it."

"Maybe, but the mere existence of it makes me a threat," I murmured. "They'll never take me back and if they do, I'll never belong."

"You never did anyway."

I grunted and looked through the window at the overgrown garden outside. "It doesn't matter anymore. That part of my life is over."

"Because of me."

"You saved my life *twice*. I could hardly leave you out there."

"I had nothing to lose."

I glanced at his chest. "Except your life."

His fingers brushed against my leg. "I saw a pretty Natural in a nightclub. Can you blame me?"

I raised my eyebrows. "Pretty?"

"*Beautiful.*"

No one had ever called me pretty before, let alone beautiful. A flush crept onto my cheeks and I tried to hide behind a curtain of inky black hair.

"Don't," Elijah whispered. "You don't have to hide from me."

My throat tightened and I forced my gaze to meet his.

"No one's ever wanted to help me," something unspoken passed between us, "until you."

My heart leapt and I drew in a shaky breath. My emotions took hold and I leaned down, pressing my lips against his.

For a fraction of a second, I thought I'd read him wrong, but as he returned my kiss, a trillion tiny fireworks exploded across my skin. I recklessly deepened our embrace and lost myself in his taste.

It was true no one had ever called me beautiful, but no one had ever kissed me, either. A demon had the pleasure and for once in my damned life, *I didn't care.*

I drew back, allowing myself to study his features. Tracing the curve of his jaw with shaking fingers, I relished the feel of his stubble and the rise and fall of his lips.

"We can go anywhere," he whispered. "We can leave them all behind and *live.*"

I trembled at the thought. "What about your cure?"

"We can look for it elsewhere. The Naturals will never help us."

I wanted to say yes, but too many doubts held me back. He couldn't take away a lifetime of training and dismiss the mystery of his past with one kiss. Now I understood how people made rash decisions under the influence of lust—it was more addictive than anything I'd ever felt.

"I know it's hard," he went on. "Being a Natural is all you've ever known, but there's an entire world out there, Madeleine, and we can be in it."

"Shh…" I murmured, "you're delirious."

"I've never been clearer. My demon side…" he coughed, grimacing at the movement, "is busy right now."

I shook my head. "I barely know you."

His fingers stroked through the curtain of my inky black hair. "You know more than you realise."

"You keep saying that, but I've yet to see it."

"You will…"

Sighing, I looked around the cottage. I needed to breathe.

I fell back to my training and realised we'd need supplies if we were going to stay here for another day or two. I'd checked all the cupboards last night, and apart from some odd pieces of linen and dishes over the sink, there was no food. Elijah needed to keep up his strength if he had any chance of fighting off his infection. As soon as he was able—and when the search had died down—we'd leave.

"I'm going out to find us some food," I told him.

"You can't," he said, his eyes flashing. "The hills will be crawling with Naturals."

I rolled my eyes. "I'll be fine. If you hadn't noticed, your Darkness is barely keeping your fever down. You need to eat. Besides, we need bandages and antiseptic."

He snorted, unimpressed.

"I'll be back soon, okay?"

"You're always so much fun," he said, his eyes drooping as his fever drew him back to sleep.

"Yeah…" I murmured, brushing my hand over his brow, "I hear I'm a real riot."

⸻

I eyed the small Off-Licence in the centre of the village. I knelt behind a garbage bin and a shrub, my nose itching from the stench of rotten rubbish. A life of excitement and adventure, huh?

The village was a sleepy little hamlet and nothing much stirred it from its slumber besides the odd passing car. At least there was nothing supernatural lurking—a small win.

I checked my cloak, knowing it'd conceal me from human eyes. It was firmly in place, but it wouldn't help me one iota if I stumbled across a Natural. The Light and Dark could see through the flimsy illusion, though it was essential for keeping our comings and goings from the outside world.

I'd be lying if I said Elijah's human side didn't excite me. He'd put forth a tantalising dream, but once his mutation returned to regular airtime, the bubble would burst. I didn't have many other choices and the ones I did sucked.

I watched a human man walk down the footpath towards the Off-Licence. When it was clear he was going inside, I shot out from behind the bin and darted across the street. I slipped through the door behind him like a devious fox, careful not to step on his heels.

A man was behind the counter, reading a newspaper and lifted his head.

"Good morning," he said to the customer I'd ghosted behind.

"Hiya, Albert."

I ignored their conversation and ducked into one

of three narrow aisles, thankful for my cloak. No one else was in the store, otherwise I'd be inside the world's most irritating obstacle course.

"Frank said he saw a creature up on the hill the other night," the shopkeeper said to the customer. "A big slimy thing, he said."

"Frank is a closet alcoholic," the man said dismissively. "He'd see a sheep in the dark and think it was Big Foot."

"People have said they've seen UFOs around here."

"Albert, you can't be serious! UFOs?"

That was one thing that amused me about making myself invisible. Overhearing human conversations was…*enlightening*. The big slimy creature was worrying, though. If humans were seeing demons around Camelot—

I shook my head. It wasn't my concern anymore.

Tuning out their conversation, I snatched up a reusable shopping bag and began to fill it, watching the shopkeeper and his friend as they debated the possibilities of extra-terrestrial life. Shoplifting seemed the lesser of the evils I'd committed, so I didn't bat an eyelid as I pinched a variety of crackers, rice cakes, long life milk, powdered soup, and instant noodles.

Finally, I stopped by the medicine and looked for some ointment and bandages—anything that could help Elijah. Double-checking the two men at the counter, I pilfered some antiseptic, gauze, and a few packets of ibuprofen.

I waited at the front of the store until a woman

opened the door. She stepped inside and I ducked through the gap unseen, guilt over my haul following me outside.

A dark figure loomed across the street and my senses went haywire. Ducking behind the bushes beside the store, I stared through the illusion as a second figure joined the first.

Trent.

He sensed me, our familiarity drawing his gaze. We stared at one another for a long moment before he turned to his partner—a Natural who'd stood behind Rhys and joined in on his disgusting chant.

"Take the north side," Trent told him. "I'll check the south and meet you back here in fifteen."

"You got it." The Natural moved down the lane between the café and the grocer. Once Trent was alone, he strode across the street, a look of pure anger on his face.

When he was in range, he grabbed my arm and jerked me behind the bush and out of sight. I dropped my stolen bag of groceries and wrenched away.

"What the hell are you playing at?" he demanded. "The entire camp is searching for you. It was all Aiden could do to stop his brother from putting out a kill order."

"Hello to you, too," I drawled.

"Give me one reason I shouldn't drag your arse back to Camelot."

"I'm not going to betray the Light to the Dark," I told him. "I had to leave. You know what would have happened to me."

His frown deepened. "Exile."

"I just want to disappear, Trent. I don't belong with the Naturals anymore. I haven't since—"

"*You're wrong.*"

"It doesn't matter now, does it?"

"*Light help me.*" He shook his head, enraged. "Madeleine… How did you get past Thompson's Light? They're saying you had help from…" He couldn't say the word *demon*.

I ground my teeth together as my mutation struggled against my Light. I couldn't make Trent an accomplice to my betrayal. Just telling him the truth would implicate him, because I knew he'd do whatever it took to protect me—that's the kind of standup guy he was. I couldn't let him screw up his life because of my stupidity.

"Tell Aiden I suspect the building he unearthed is important to the Dark."

"What are you talking about?"

"I think the Balan captured me to get to it, or at least something inside Camelot. They'll try again. Humans are already starting to notice."

"Madel—"

Before he could get out another syllable, I struck him in the temple. The blow flattened him, and he crumpled to the ground in an unconscious heap. I hadn't graduated top of our class for nothing.

I snatched up the bag of food and sprinted down the lane, then vaulted over the fence. I checked for a tail, but I was clear. Not taking my stroke of luck for granted, I didn't stop running until I reached the cottage.

Pushing the front door open, I called for Elijah. "We need to move," I said, dumping the bag onto the floor. "They're in the village. It's only a matter of time before they—"

I froze, my gaze falling on Elijah. His skin had a sickly grey sheen and the wounds in his chest looked red and angry as if they'd opened up again.

"Madeleine," he rasped, "you need to leave me behind."

"No…" I shook my head.

"Madeleine, I can smell the infection."

I fell to my knees beside the bed, barely holding back my tears. "I can't leave you behind. *I won't.*"

"*Please.* I'll be dead by nightfall." He coughed, his eyes drooping. "Go before they capture you. *Go…*"

Unconsciousness took him and I grasped his hand. It was true I'd risked everything for him, but it wasn't because of his stupid binding. He was just trying to become human again. And…

And I cared for him.

If I wanted to save his life, I had to do something now. This mess had grown beyond me and Elijah. Running away was a bad idea, even though the thought of exploring the world had excited me.

No matter how far we roamed, I couldn't escape the fact that I owed everything to the Naturals. Arondight had saved my soul for Light's sake and what had I done? I couldn't leave knowing that the

Dark was bearing down on Camelot. I had friends there, no matter how few they were.

And I couldn't leave Elijah to die knowing I could have saved him.

So, I made the only choice I could.

It was my life or Elijah's…

…and I chose his.

14

———

The outer wall of Camelot was alive with Light as we approached. I could see it rippling through the night like a sheen of oil floating on top of a puddle.

Elijah's boots scraped against the trail, but he came without complaint—though he was too delirious not to.

I bit my bottom lip as I looked up at the barrier that surrounded base camp. This was new, thanks to me. There was no getting through unless I could repeat last night's performance.

I'd patched Elijah up as best I could with the bandages I'd stolen from the village, but my basic field training wouldn't hold for long. It was enough to transport him, nothing more.

We had to get through the barrier, then through the camp to the infirmary . . . both without being seen. Once there, I'd convince Ramona to help.

Elijah's only crime was being a demon and that

had been forced on him. I'd convince Ramona that his intentions were pure. I'd convince them all, even if it meant my exile.

I drew him into my web as we huddled behind an outcropping of rock. The square edges gave away that it'd once been a part of the wall, the massive block flung here when the rift had torn apart the castle and the tremors rippled through the city.

I pressed my palm against Elijah's forehead as I watched the rotation of guards on the perimeter. It felt like liquid fire was burning underneath his skin, and I knew we didn't have much time.

Taking a chance, I hauled him across the open space between the block of stone and the barrier. I reached for my mutation, disregarding the fear I had of being seduced by the seductive nature of the Dark, and allowed it to cover us.

Elijah's presence anchored me to reality and he stirred. "Madeleine?" he muttered. "Where…"

"Shh," I murmured, "it will be over soon."

Taking a deep breath, we stepped through the barrier. Light tickled my face, tendrils sticking to my skin like the gossamer of a delicate spider's web. I blinked, dazed by the sight of the base camp before us. It was familiar, but alien all at the same time.

I slammed my Light down around my mutation, cutting it off before it could ruin my life with its sarcastic comebacks.

"Welcome to Camelot," I muttered as Elijah slumped against me.

The infirmary was located three rows down and

two tents across. I dragged Elijah into the shadows behind the first khaki-coloured monstrosity. From memory, it wasn't occupied being on the outer edges.

Ahead, a male Natural dressed in head to toe black tactical gear rounded the corner. My eyes widened and I backed against the wall, my heart pounding. Elijah's knees buckled as my gaze dropped to the arondight blade at the guy's belt. If I was quick…

The Natural jogged past us, never breaking his stride. His gaze fixed ahead and never strayed towards us. It was as if we were invisible.

Elijah groaned, but the soldier was already far enough away from our position that he didn't hear.

Across from us, a tent flap swung open and a woman slipped through. She hefted a box in her arms and her gaze swept past us like my ability encased us in empty air.

No one could see us.

But that was impossible. Naturals could see through a cloak and so could demons. Something wasn't right about this, but I wasn't going to take it for granted.

I understood whatever I was doing was a unique ability, one the Naturals wouldn't take kindly to— impervious to Light, immune to Dark. I hoped my current theory was wrong.

I cursed and shook my head. I was already referring to my people like I wasn't one of them anymore. What was I now that the enemy had awoken my Dark side? A hybrid, I supposed.

Anchoring Elijah against me, I held him steady with my Light and forged through the camp, no longer worried about being seen.

Dragging Elijah into the infirmary, I saw Ramona sitting at the opposite end of the tent, bent over a microscope.

"Ramona."

At the unexpected sound of my voice, she shot to her feet and stared at us. "What the…"

I eased Elijah onto the closest bed. "I need your help. His wounds are infected and—"

She strode across the tent and pushed me aside, dragging me away from the bed. "What have you done?" she demanded. "Everyone is out hunting you. If they—"

"Ramona," I snapped, "he's dying."

She blinked and looked down at Elijah as I eased him out of his T-shirt. He was barely conscious, pain the only thing keeping him tethered to life. The trek here had only been a few miles, but the toll had been high.

"A demon attacked him," I told her as I uncovered my hasty bandaging. "If it was a Balan or one of those things that captured me, I'm not sure. He didn't say."

"How long has he been like this?"

"Since last night."

She shook her head in disbelief. "How is he still alive?" Clucking her tongue, she leaned over Elijah and pressed her palm against his brow. The moment her skin came into contact with his, she snatched her hand away as if it had been burnt. "He's—"

"A demon," I finished for her. "Though his humanity remains."

"How did you find him?"

"It's a long story," I muttered.

"Long enough that you never reported it, I assume."

"No one would have believed my intentions were for the Light, even if I did."

"*Madeleine*, that's no excuse for lying on your mission reports!"

"What did you expect?" I exclaimed. "Everyone treats me like I'm a leper! Of course, I'll keep it a secret! Do you realise how this looks for me?"

"After all we've been through, you could have come to me."

I bristled, barely holding onto my frustrated tears. "I couldn't and you know it. I tried to convince him to come, but he wouldn't step foot inside Camelot. You know why? Because he knew he'd be carved open and studied. People like us will always be outside the Light, no matter how much we want to be a part of it. Human Convergence stole my life and it stole Elijah's."

"It's not that simple, Madeleine," Ramona argued. "The Dark is all-consuming."

"He saved my life," I said, seething. "What was I supposed to do? Leave him to die? He was attacked because he helped me escape from Ben Nevis."

Ramona sighed. "Ethically, maybe you were right.

But you conspired with the enemy, Madeleine. The Codex is clear about our stance towards the Dark."

"He's a victim, Ramona, just like I was. You can't tell me you didn't feel it when you touched him. The line isn't as clear cut as it used to be."

She lowered her gaze and studied Elijah. "What's the end game here, Madeleine? What does he want?"

"*A cure.*"

"Are you sure about that?"

"Yes!" I threw my hands into the air. "Are you going to help him or not? While we argue about stupid ethics, the infection is killing him." Unbidden tears welled in my eyes. "Ramona, *please.*"

She stared at me open-mouthed. "You care for him. A demon?"

"Crucify me later," I pleaded. "*Please, help him.*"

Scowling, she pushed me aside and began to inspect Elijah's wounds. Without a word, she began to administer her Light, searching out the limits of the infection.

"It's not good," she told me. "But I don't think it's too late."

I sighed in relief and sank onto the neighbouring bed. Exhaustion was tugging at me beyond the reaches of my Light and I was long past caring what Ramona thought of me. Admitting I felt empathy for a demon was one of the worst things I could admit to, but it wasn't all of Elijah. *She'd see.*

"I can do some non-invasive preliminary tests," Ramona told me as she prepared to treat Elijah's infection, "but I can't hide you both for long."

"Do what you can."

I watched Ramona's every move as she administered antibiotics to combat the poison that was leeching into Elijah's body.

She conducted her tests while we waited for the medicine to do its work. She took some of his blood and peered at it under a microscope, then used her Light to manipulate the cells before looking again.

She returned to him several times, checking on his infection and to take scans and make other assessments. I did not understand what half of them were, even though I'd likely gone through the same process as a teenager.

"Can you help him?" I asked when I couldn't take it anymore.

Ramona shook her head. "I've tried multiple simulations, but I'm afraid the mutation has taken over."

"It can't have," I argued. "I could see him switch between two different halves…" I looked up at her, pleading. "I saw it, Ramona."

She turned back to the tablet, but it was only a tactic to stall so she could gather her thoughts.

"It must be a different strain," she mused, flicking her finger across the tablet screen. Numbers and diagrams flashed past, but they meant nothing to me. "But I can't see where it differentiates between what he once was and what he is now in the results. This thing has completely taken over. That's the only conclusion I can come to, or—"

"Or what?"

"Or he wasn't human to begin with."

A lump formed in my throat and I swallowed hard. "If he wasn't human, then what was he?"

Her gaze met mine, troubled. "I don't know."

If she was right, then that's why he wasn't cured when Mordred died. It just didn't add up. Our world was comprised of Naturals, demons, and humans. Nothing else remained after the cataclysm.

"I think it's time you told me everything, Madeleine," Ramona said, setting down the tablet. "And leave nothing out this time, because I know you're still not revealing everything."

I gritted my teeth. She was right, but a small part of me hoped that when the Regula was called to haul my arse to prison, they wouldn't detect my mutation.

"Will he live?" I asked, lifting my gaze.

She nodded. "Yes, but I cannot guarantee his ongoing safety."

"I understand."

I watched the rise and fall of Elijah's chest as he slept. His wounds looked better already. He'd bear the scars for the rest of his existence, but I hoped he'd agree it was a small price to pay.

Ramona sat beside me and placed her hand on my shoulder, her Light rippling through me. "Oh, Madeleine…"

And with that simple touch, she knew the truth about me.

"I'm sorry," she said. "I wish I could help you."

"What do you mean?" I asked, my brow creasing.

"I know your mutation," she murmured. "We

spent all that time together, working to stop it from spreading. I studied it for a year trying to find a cure. I synthesised every scenario I could before Mordred's death."

I sucked in a shaky breath. "There was never going to be a cure for Human Convergence, was there?"

"No, but…"

"But what?"

"I don't need to do a test to know your mutation has changed." She turned so she faced me. "Madeleine, your mutation has fused with your soul."

I jerked to my feet and shook my head. "You're lying."

"Thirty years of studying soul medicine has taught me how to diagnose with a simple brush of Light. I can feel it in you."

"*No.*"

"I'm so sorry," she said, her eyes misting with tears. "Madeleine…there is nothing that can cure this."

I collapsed next to Elijah and took his hand in mine. He was completely out to it and not even my touch stirred him.

"What about him?" I demanded.

"Perhaps, in time, he can return to what he once was."

I knew when I walked into Camelot, there was no leaving, but I attempted to hatch a plan anyway. Elijah might not get his cure, but we could escape this place with both our lives intact. The world awaited us, just like he'd said. We could still go.

"Promise me you'll help him," I said to Ramona.

She stood beside us. "You know I can't. If the Regula judge him to be an innocent, then I will do whatever I can to help him. Until then, I can only see to his wounds."

The Regula wouldn't do shite for Elijah if my experience was anything to go by. They'd look at him and see Darkness, disregarding what he was before. I saved his life, only to condemn him to his worst fears.

Ramona stirred behind me. "You love him, don't you?"

I sniffed, holding back a flood of tears. "I don't know what love is," I whispered. How could I when I didn't know who I was?

Who am I?

I was the Light in the dark and the Dark in the light. The Codex—the book that decreed all Natural law—didn't allow for shades of grey. That's what I was now…a shadow.

"*And so, the battle lines are drawn,*" I whispered.

Stomping boots thundered into the infirmary behind me and I tightened my grip on Elijah's hand.

"I'll come back for you," I whispered, my Light brushing against him. "*I promise.* Then we'll be free, just like you said we would. *I understand now.*"

"Madeleine Greenbriar," Caleb Thompson bellowed, "you're under arrest."

15

____

They found a more secure place to lock me up this time around.

A windowless stone room somewhere within the boundary of Camelot was my prison—cold, damp, and cut off from the outside world. I lost all sense of time. Day, night, who knew how long I'd been here. It could have been few hours or a few days for all I knew.

I sat in the far corner, my head resting against freezing stone. My fingers stroked a clump of moss beside my boot, but no matter how hard I tried, I couldn't stop the voices in my head.

Darkness was in my soul.

It taunted me, calling out to my despair. Playing on my guilt. Tempting me to fall into its all-consuming blackness.

I wouldn't give it the satisfaction.

My hand found the hilt of my arondight blade, surprised they hadn't taken it away. It could only

165

mean Ramona hadn't told them about me yet, and I was thankful for the small kindness. I'd tell Aiden and Thompson the truth on my own terms.

A drop of water slapped on my head and I swiped my hand through my hair. Another cage. At least this one didn't come with a meat closet.

I slid to the side, manoeuvring out of the drip-zone.

Ramona's diagnosis was a shock, but it explained why I could get through the camp unseen, but not how Trent had spotted me in the village. Maybe he could pierce my cloak because deep down, I wanted him to see me. He'd fought for me after all . . . and I'd repaid him with a fist to the temple.

Elijah…

I didn't know if he lived, if he was free, if he'd been granted asylum, or if he'd escaped. He hadn't tried to contact me via our bond at all.

I'm sorry. I tried to do the right thing. I didn't want you to die. I wanted to give you a future.

I pressed my forehead against my knees and swallowed my tears.

Stone scraped against stone, rousing me from my shame spiral and I rose to my feet, searching for the source of the sound. My limbs were stiff and my body felt chilled all the way through. Hunger tugged at my stomach, but I wouldn't allow physical discomfort to become a weakness.

Light shone through a gap in the wall, and another scrape opened the crack farther. Then a familiar face peered into my prison.

Aiden.

He looked at me as if he'd just arrived at my funeral. Saying nothing, he gestured for me to come, stepping back as I approached. So this was how it was going to be now. I'd lost everyone who'd ever fought for me. I looked within and there was nothing inside me.

I emerged into the day, blinking as my eyes adjusted to the sunlight, ready to face whatever awaited me with my head held high.

I felt his presence before I saw him.

Wilder stood in the centre of the square, his hands shoved deep into the pockets of his black overcoat. The Inquisitor was the picture of bureaucratic power in his fancy clothes, but the collar was flipped up as a nod to his former self—the rebellious Natural who'd fought against authority. Now, he was every part a Pendragon. All that was missing was a crown to call him King.

A dozen Naturals had lined up behind him, their arondight blades in their hands. I stared at them, shock sending a coldness through my veins. What in the Light did they think I was going to do?

Wilder's presence was overwhelming, and I almost lowered my gaze under the pressure of his. The Inquisitor's silver eyes weren't the same as Elijah's. I was looking at the Argent Flame, Excalibur, and right now, he was barely holding onto his rage.

What a disappointment I must be to him.

Aiden stepped forwards. "Wilder, I—"

The Inquisitor held up his hand, silencing his protests. "Leave us."

I caught Aiden's eye and nodded. I'd sacrificed myself to save Elijah and this was my moment of reckoning. I had to face it alone.

The Naturals retreated, leaving the square. Wilder stepped towards me, the air shimmering in his wake. As he loomed over me, silver Light fell around us in a curtain.

I breathed deeply, crippled by an influx of emotions—guilt, temptation, shame, desperation.

"Madeleine," Wilder said, the sound of his voice reverberated against the sparkling dome around us.

My bottom lip trembled as I tried to contain my shadow.

"You've broken almost all the covenants in the Codex," he seethed. "Even Scarlett wasn't this reckless."

"Maybe those bigots were right," I told him. "I'm a perverted demon-hybrid who's going to kill us all."

"Madeleine." His brow creased as he paced back and forth within the dome. "I can scarcely count the number of insurrections you've committed since your arrival at Camelot. Your capture was unfortunate, and leaving the boundary of Camelot could have been overlooked as a side effect of your echoes, but attacking a fellow Natural…" He hissed, his Flame simmering. His skin crackled with white-hot sparks as he stared at me. "You escaped your confinement, attacked a Natural in a human village, and returned with a mortally wounded demon."

"Elijah is a victim," I snapped, my power wrestling against my control. "He's not the enemy. He saved my life more than once. I'll say the same thing I said to Ramona—I couldn't repay his sacrifice with death."

"He's a demon, Madeline," Wilder stated. "Demons manipulate and lie to get what they want. He's using you to get into Camelot."

"How do you know?" I demanded. "Have you spoken to him?"

"I don't need to. There's only one thing he can be." He glanced over his shoulder. "I can feel his presence. He's not possessed, and we eradicated Human Convergence with the death of Mordred."

"You didn't."

He strode across the uneven ground and stopped in front of me. "Are you questioning me?"

"Someone has to," I replied, jutting out my chin. "Power has gone to your head, Wilder. I don't even recognise you anymore. You look tired, you know."

His lips thinned and I knew I'd hit one of his carefully guarded buttons. My mutation gurgled, excited by the prospect. His power wasn't infinite.

"What details did you leave out of your capture?" he demanded.

"I can't be sure of my allegations, but I believe the Balan wants something inside Camelot," I replied, compelled to answer as a Natural. "I assumed they would use me to get to it, but Elijah helped me escape before they could torture me into compliance."

"And what was his reasoning for helping you?" he demanded. "Demons always have a price."

"Elijah's conditions were to assist him in finding a cure for his mutation. Nothing more."

"And why didn't he come to us?"

"Because he believed we would treat him with open hostility and cut him up into little pieces to study exactly what he is."

"We always help those who seek out the Light," Wilder stated, quoting the Codex.

"His fears are my reality," I snapped. "You of all people should understand. You faced a lifetime of prejudice, but you turned out to be Excalibur. I didn't."

"This isn't the same. That demon is in full control of his actions. You weren't."

"That's shite and you know it," I exclaimed. "Our world isn't just Light and Dark anymore. They're evolving to survive."

"What are you saying?" Wilder demanded.

"I'm saying that Elijah and I are the same. The haters were right about me, I just didn't know it until they captured me."

"You're—"

"A demon-hybrid."

"Impossible." He shook his head, shocked. "If you had a live mutation, I'd be able to sense it."

"Maybe Excalibur isn't as absolute as everyone wishes you were." I held out my hand. "Go on. See for yourself."

Wilder slid his palm against mine and I felt his

power reach out. The moment it connected, he jerked his hand away and stared at me, celestial Flame simmering in his eyes.

"Madeleine…"

"Scarlett saved my soul, but Mordred's death didn't eradicate my mutation. Out of all the Naturals who were altered, I was the only one who wasn't completely taken over. Those that were, kept their souls, right?"

"It latched onto your soul when Scarlett…" Wilder shook his head in disbelief.

"You saved my Light when you killed Mordred, but the mutation never left. It lay dormant until they activated it—a precursor to the evolution we're seeing now," I replied. "Which means this is who I am, and it's not going to change. Not even the mighty Excalibur can free my soul and return me to the Light."

When it came down to basic DNA, I didn't even think I was the same as Elijah. He'd been altered either through possession or in a laboratory, while an accident created me. Scarlett had the best intentions when she saved my life, but no one knew what would ultimately become of me.

I was a bridge between two worlds, a connection between night and day. One that could be used for good…or evil.

Elijah's words from the road in the Highlands came back to me and I almost crumpled to my knees before the Inquisitor. He had been trying to force me to open my mind and evolve because he'd known what I was all along. I'd gotten a taste of it when I nullified Thompson's barrier and now, I knew my soul had been irreversibly altered.

I was a shadow—neither Light nor Dark. If I could develop my power and evolve…then no one could stop me.

In the wrong hands, I had the potential to become a weapon of mass destruction.

"I'm left with no other choice." Wilder held his hand out, palm up. "Hand over your arondight blade."

"Do you understand what I've become?" I whispered.

"Yes." There was a note of sadness in his voice, but he didn't back down.

I slipped my arondight hilt from my belt and placed it in Wilder's palm. If Elijah was right, I never needed it, but its loss was akin to losing a limb. "Do with me what you will but know I'm the only person who can help you find what the Dark is looking for."

"The time for bargaining is over," Wilder stated. "I will pass final judgment in due course."

"Elijah was only looking for help," I said. "Please don't punish him for my insurrections. Remember that I came willingly."

The Inquisitor's expression gave away nothing. He lifted his hand and the dome shimmered and dissolved, returning us to the full view of Camelot.

Trent and another Natural emerged from a side alley and each took one of my arms, firmly holding me. I knew it was all for show. Wilder understood I could fight back and likely win, but if I tried to resist, Elijah's fate would be sealed.

"Return Greenbriar to her cell," the Inquisitor ordered.

I didn't fight. They dragged me back to the stone room to await sentencing. Who knew what I'd face when they decided. Life imprisonment in the Glastonbury catacombs and stripped of my Light was the best I could hope for. Knowing what I'd become, I wasn't even sure they could take my power away.

I caught Trent's gaze, but there was nothing there. Empty words wouldn't fix my betrayal of our friendship. He was lost to me, as were my people, my home, and my family.

There was nothing else to say as they slid the stone over the opening, closing me inside my prison.

Darkness of another kind took me, obliterating all hope from my heart.

I was alone.

My Light staved off the chill of my dark prison, but it didn't warm my heart.

If they ruled me to be a threat to the balance, I'd be executed. I couldn't see any other outcome. Imprisonment would be a kindness. In the current climate of increased demonic activity around Camelot, the Regula would want to take a tough stance against insurrection.

Stone scraped against stone and light flooded my cage.

Maisy stepped through the gap, a tray in her hands. The smell of hot food wafted in with the breeze, filling the small space to the brim.

"Maisy," I murmured.

She looked down at me and set the tray onto a stone block. "I brought you something to eat."

"Is Elijah…" I wasn't sure if I should ask, but I was desperate to know if he lived.

Her eyebrows rose. "You want to know about your demon?"

"Yes."

"He lives," she said with a sigh. "Ramona healed his wounds and they have restrained him until the Regula can rule on his fate."

"He's alive?" I let my head fall into my hands and swallowed a sob. There was hope after all.

"What is it about him?" Maisy asked, distaste clear in her voice. "I was in the infirmary for two seconds and his Darkness made me sick to the stomach."

I fisted my hands in my hair. How was I ever going to find a place amongst the Naturals if that's how they looked at Elijah? He was a victim, but the way Maisy spoke about him made it sound as if he'd chosen to become Dark.

"If Elijah hadn't rescued me from that Balan demon, I would've been forced to the Dark by now," I snapped. "He saved me from a fate worse than death. How could I not repay that debt?" I looked up at her, disappointed that some of her old tendencies were showing.

"Why him?" she asked. "Why a demon?"

"Because I saw myself in him," I replied. "They altered him against his will, just like me. He didn't choose to be what he is. He just wanted to find a cure."

"People are saying you're a demon again. That it's why the Inquisitor is here."

I had nothing to hide anymore. Despite our rocky

past and my betrayal, Maisy was my friend. I owed her the truth, even if it meant she'd walk out of this prison hating me.

"I can't be saved, Maisy." I shook my head as a tear rolled down my cheek. "My mutation never went away. A small piece of it latched onto my soul and… The Dark activated it when they captured me."

She drew in a shaky breath. "What are you saying?"

"I'm not a demon or a Natural. I'm… Well, I don't know what I am exactly. I'm half and half. A hybrid."

"That's how you escaped?"

I nodded. "I walked through Thompson's barrier like it wasn't even there."

"That means…" she trailed off, but she didn't have to finish her thought. She understood that I could get up and walk out of Camelot any time I chose. "Then why are you still here? After the way we've treated you, I wouldn't be surprised if you left."

"The Naturals are my people," I replied. "Well, you were. This was my whole life. Everything I was, everything I dedicated myself to, was to the Light. I tried to get past what happened at the Academy, but I think a part of me always knew there was no going back. The bullying, the taunts, the loneliness, the struggle… Everything they said about me was true, but I never worked for the Dark. How could I?"

Maisy sighed and looked through the opening of my prison to where Camelot stood silent vigil.

"I'm sorry for what happened to you, Madeleine,"

she murmured. "I really am. I know it wasn't your fault."

"What's going to happen to me?"

She shrugged. "I don't know. After Wilder spoke to you, he went to the castle and hasn't returned."

That didn't bode well.

"Tell Trent I'm sorry for hitting him," I murmured. "And tell Aiden I'm sorry for… Well, tell him that I'm just sorry for everything."

"Me too," Maisy said, turning away. "And Madeleine?"

I looked up to find her lingering at the door, silhouetted by the sun.

"Are you still in there?" she whispered.

"Yes," I told her, "I am."

She smiled. "Then never forget it."

Chicken drumsticks, string beans, and boiled potatoes. Maisy had brought me decent food considering my predicament, but no knife and fork. I snorted at the irony.

My eyes were adjusting to the dark like they never had before. It was unnatural and slightly worrying, but handy considering I was locked in a lightless stone room. I wondered what else I could do if I put my back into it. Elijah kept hinting at evolution, but I wasn't sure this was what he had in mind.

I picked up a potato and threw it across the room with a frustrated cry. The old Madeleine Greenbriar would never sit here marinating in her melancholy. She'd get up off her sorry arse and flip the bird at the nearest authority figure, then do whatever it took to get the job done.

I was as good as dead, so what did it matter? Nothing was stopping me from walking out of this stupid city, nothing at all.

If I stayed here, I'd be locked away forever. If I had the power to stand against the Dark, maybe I could make a difference before the shit hit the fan. They wanted to take Camelot back and with Elijah's help, we could figure out what they wanted before it became a problem. I was the only person alive who could walk into the Balan's lair and stop another war from erupting.

Despite what I'd become and how my own people had treated me, I was still on the side of good and that had to count for something.

I stood with renewed hope and pressed my palms against the door. The catch was I had to do it without tipping too far into the Dark. And not get caught. And not hurt anyone—at least not too much.

After all those years at the Academy listening to lectures about 'the balance', and trying not to fall asleep with boredom, here I was relying on the fine line between good and evil more than ever. Oh man, I wished I'd taken more notes.

There was only one way to find out if this was going to work, so I took a deep and let go.

My mutation rushed outwards and I lashed at it

with my Light. Silver tendrils wrapped around the red fingers of Darkness, fusing them together.

Sweat beaded across my forehead and I moaned softly, scraping my fingernails against the stone wall. Was this what accepting fate felt like? My mutation had been reaching out all this time, wanting to join with my Light, except I couldn't keep calling it 'my mutation'.

The two energies flowed together—it filled my limbs and mixed with my blood. I was being born again, my soul accepting what it had become…all so I could save Elijah's life and stop the Dark.

I opened my eyes, my heart filled with renewed purpose, and I pushed aside the stone that was blocking the entrance to my prison.

As I stepped into the square, the guards drew their arondight blades, sparks skidding across stone. They were watching the opening behind me as I approached, unaware that I was already before them.

Knowing I couldn't leave them conscious, I slipped between the two men and struck—they never stood a chance. With two quick blows, they slumped to the ground, their swords clattering against stone.

Leaving them where they lay, I walked through the lower city, my gaze darting around as if I was seeing life for the first time.

I wasn't far from base camp. I could feel the ebb of Light from here, the concentration of Naturals creating a beacon. Strange, I hadn't noticed it before.

Shrugging it off as a side effect of levelling up my

power reserves, I made my way towards the camp where Elijah was.

The mood in the little khaki-coloured city was sombre as I walked unseen through the tents. Conversations ebbed and flowed, all of them talking about me and Wilder's appearance at Camelot. Maisy was right—he'd gone up to the castle the day before and hadn't returned.

I was concerned, but he was our leader—not to mention one half of the most powerful duo our kind had ever encountered. He'd be fine.

Two guards stood outside the infirmary, standing watch over their prisoner within. I approached them, willing myself into a pocket of space beyond their vision. Then I simply walked past them and into the infirmary.

Elijah lay in the bed where I'd left him days before. Standing over him, I noticed his colour was better and though his wounds were bound, the bandages didn't show any signs of blood.

It also didn't take a rocket scientist to see they'd doped him up to the eyeballs. I pulled back the bandages and found three red scars slashing across his chest from shoulder to ribs. Ramona had lived up to her promise and spectacularly, too.

Elijah began to stir, sensing my touch.

"Hey," he rasped through the fog of sedation, "pretty Natural."

"Thank the Light you're not dead."

"Your friends did a good job," he murmured, his

eyes drooping. "They also know how to incapacitate a guy like me really well. Give her a gold star."

"Still a smart arse, I see."

"Imagine my surprise when I woke up in Camelot," he drawled. "You promised not to bring me here."

"I did no such thing." I wrapped my hands around his head and circled my thumbs over his temples.

"Mmm…" he murmured. "Am I at a day spa?"

I rolled my eyes and concentrated. A sedative Light manipulation was wrapped around his mind like a blanket that locked away his Darkness, but it wasn't the only thing that kept him subdued. Someone had tethered him to the infirmary—most likely Wilder. It wouldn't be pretty if Elijah left the boundary.

The Lady of the Lake gave the Naturals their power. She was the same celestial being who'd gifted Excalibur—otherwise known as Wilder Pendragon— and Arondight theirs. We were all made of the same energy, just in different quantities. That meant I could nullify my way through Elijah's sedation and get us out of Camelot, just like I'd gotten us in.

I reached out, my power merging with the sedation. My fingers began to tingle as the Light dissolved around Elijah's mind. Then, it was gone.

He jerked upright, wide-eyed and alert. "Madeline."

I looked into his steely eyes and was glad to see him return to his old self.

"You're breaking me out?" His lips tugged up at one side. He really was roguishly handsome.

"Stay with me and no one will stop us," I told him.

He stilled, his gaze piercing mine. "You know, don't you?"

"The truth about my mutation? Oh yeah, do I ever." He slid his legs out of bed and I dumped his clothes next to him. I pulled his socks onto his feet as he fumbled with his T-shirt. "You knew all this time and couldn't tell me?"

"I suspected," he replied, his voice muffled by the fabric as he dragged his T-shirt over his body. "But I had no way of knowing for sure."

"It doesn't matter," I said as I handed him his trousers. "Get dressed before someone comes."

"Madeleine," he grabbed my wrist, "if you do this—"

"I won't be able to do anything strapped to an autopsy table, Elijah," I interrupted.

"If we leave, then what?"

"We stop the Dark from coming back to Camelot and we find your cure." I wrenched my arm away. "Now finish getting dressed."

"Do I have a choice?"

"Of course, you do. Just admit you want to help Camelot as much as I do."

He snorted and shoved his legs into his pants. "I'll never admit anything, not after the scars your fancy doctor friend left me with."

I threw his boots at him. "Chicks dig scars."

"I assume you have a plan," he said as he laced himself in. "I like chaos as much as the next mutant, but not when we're surrounded by a hundred Naturals and a magical sword."

I rolled my eyes and pulled him close. "First of all, Excalibur is a *person*. And I don't need a plan."

He whistled. "You talk a big game."

"Just you wait."

I grabbed his hand and drew his presence against mine. The more I tested my limits, the more they seemed to expand. Piece of cake.

We stood at the opening in the tent with Wilder's barrier clearly visible. A transparent silver veil covered the exit, one that I hadn't seen when I'd walked in.

"Are you sure?" Elijah asked. "After everything I've been through, I don't want to turn into a pile of ash."

"I'm sure."

He screwed up his nose at the two Naturals who were standing to attention with their backs to us. "What about the guards?" he whispered.

"I told you. Stay with me and no one will stop us."

He grunted and narrowed his eyes in challenge. To prove my point, I dragged him out of the infirmary, past the guards, and down the row of tents until we reached the outer edge of the camp. The outer wall loomed before us and all we had to do was keep walking and we'd be free.

"Stop," Trent called after us and we froze.

"I thought you had this invisibility thing down," Elijah hissed.

"Uh, I guess not." It was far more likely that deep down, I desperately wanted Trent's forgiveness, just like I secretly wanted him to see me back in the village. What unfortunate timing for a loophole to reveal itself.

We turned to find Trent a few paces behind, with his arondight blade drawn. The sword glowed with silver Light as he pointed the tip at us. His warning was clear.

I stepped in front of Elijah, shielding him from my friend—at least I hoped he was still my friend somewhere underneath all that anger.

"We just want to be free," I murmured. "We don't want to cause any trouble."

"You made your choice, Madeleine," Trent spat. "You chose a demon over your people."

I shook my head. "I helped an innocent who risked his life to save mine."

He scowled and stepped closer, the point of his blade pressing against my throat. "You betrayed us."

Elijah hissed and I grasped his hand, silencing him.

"I may have gone about things the wrong way," I said to Trent, "but I was trying to save a life."

"And she found out who she really is," Elijah snapped.

"Shut up," Trent exclaimed, the point of his sword pricking my flesh.

"You know I can't stay here," I said, holding my hands up. "I can do more good out there than I can while I await my death sentence."

"Wilder would never execute you," he argued.

"Wilder is bound by the Codex as we all are. As the Inquisitor, he will do as it decrees."

Silently, Trent shook his head.

"I have to go," I urged. "The Dark has its eyes on Camelot and this thing inside me might stop it before whatever it is begins."

"And him?" Trent demanded.

I tightened my grip on Elijah's hand. "I will keep my promise. I will help him find a cure."

He shook his head and curled his lip. "What's stopping him from returning to the Dark and betraying us all?"

"Me," I replied.

Trent's arm began to shake, and I felt a single drop of blood trace its way down my neck.

"You know me, Trent," I murmured. "Nothing's changed other than my awareness of what I've always been."

He glanced at Elijah. "Not always."

"No," I shook my head, "just the last five years."

"Semantics," Elijah muttered.

Trent hissed and lowered his sword. "Go."

I backed way, forcing Elijah to do the same. "Thank you."

"If I see you again…"

I understood. He'd be forced to follow through on orders, no matter what they were.

I dragged Elijah away, drawing him into the embrace of my unknown power. Trent blinked and looked around in bewilderment. I knew to his eyes, we were gone. The score between us had been settled and now it was about what came next.

No one stopped us as we walked out of base camp. The barrier of Light around the outer wall was nothing more than an illusion as we stepped through to our freedom. Not even Excalibur stirred in his castle.

We were ghosts moving from one life to the next.

"Come," Elijah said as we climbed the hill hand in hand, "we have work to do."

I nodded as I glanced over my shoulder one last time, despair tugging at my heart.

Goodbye, Madeline Greenbriar, I thought. *It was fun while it lasted.*

17

We found a cheap hotel on the outskirts of Birmingham.

After a little alteration on the clerk, we got ourselves a room at the back of the building, away from other guests. I was just thankful that part of my power still worked the way it used to.

The hallways were empty, though it was past midnight. A few 'do not disturb' hangers were on the door handles as we passed, and the faint hum of televisions ebbed through the walls here and there. If it wasn't for those few indicators, it would have been easy to think the entire hotel was empty.

Our room was next to a fire escape at the end of the longest corridor known to man. I slipped the keycard into the lock and pushed the door open.

"Let me do some work next time," Elijah said, following me into the room. "You're emasculating me."

I made a face. "Threatened by women, are we?"

"What do you think? I spent the better part of the last week incapacitated."

"Glad to see you're feeling better."

I checked the bathroom, then turned on the lights. Elijah walked past me and peered out of the window at the city beyond. The lights of Birmingham were bright, the lack of complete darkness jarring after Camelot.

"You don't seem concerned about Wilder finding us," I said as he swept the blackout curtains over the view.

"Your fancy sword-man won't find anything," Elijah replied, proceeding to open and close all the drawers in the bedside tables.

Speaking of swords, I realised I was unarmed. My arondight blade was still in Camelot and I had no cold iron dagger to speak of. All I had were my new abilities.

"Shame there's two beds," he said. "I enjoy being the big spoon."

I rolled my eyes to cover my embarrassment. "Don't think me saving you is a declaration of anything."

He paused his curious searching and looked at me. "A declaration of what?"

"I'm taking a shower," I snapped.

"Can I come?" Now he was just trolling me.

"No."

He laughed, then flopped down on the bed closest to the window and picked up the TV remote. The old Elijah was back with a vengeance.

Closing the bathroom door, I listened to the hum of his channel surfing and sighed. It was going to take some getting used to travelling with a half-demon.

Stripping, I slunk into the shower and scrubbed the filth of my prison off my skin. The water beat down on my back, soothing the pain and stress of the past week from my mind.

What was I? I'd become something dangerous, that much was clear. Even Wilder seemed afraid of my potential and he was the embodiment of celestial power.

Light couldn't stop me, neither could Darkness. That kind of power was unfathomable—there had to be a loophole. Nothing was absolute.

I shook my head and turned off the taps. Everyone I'd ever known hated me, and if they didn't hate me, they feared me. I didn't know which was worse. How had I become the enemy in my own story?

I stepped out of the shower and lingered in front of the mirror. Sweeping my palm across the condensation on the mirror, I stared at my reflection. My black hair was wet and stringy, my skin white and sallow, and my eyes… I blinked as the blue in my irises shimmered—red, silver, then dulled to grey. I rubbed my fists against my eyes and leaned closer to the mirror. Still grey like a monochrome pencil drawing.

The old Madeleine was dead and whoever was looking back at me was being reborn.

I emerged from the bathroom in a waft of steam, wrapped in one of the fluffy hotel bathrobes.

Elijah was where I'd left him, watching an infomercial on television, but there was a pile of clothes on the bed I hadn't seen before.

"What's that?" I asked. He'd been up to something while I was contemplating my terrible life choices in the shower. Trickery and chaos were in his nature, after all.

"While you were using up all the hot water, I glamoured some clean clothes out of the neighbours."

"Elijah." I picked up the jeans—which turned out to be an extremely convincing pair of jeggings—and scowled. "If we're going to stick together, you need to stop stealing things."

"Why? Humanity is crippled by consumerism. Most of the things they buy they don't even need. Think of the environment."

I shook my head and pulled on the jeggings, shimmying them on under the robe. We didn't have time to wait around for my clothes to dry, so I was forced to accept Elijah's stolen bounty.

He switched the TV off and grinned as I turned my back to put on the long-sleeved T-shirt. "Glad to see we're on the same page."

"I'll find a way to pay it forwards."

"Ever the Natural." He smirked. "I forgot to get you a bra."

I threw the bathrobe at his face. "No, you didn't."

He caught it with a chuckle and tossed it onto the floor. "You're too clever for me."

I lowered my gaze, imagining I could see his scars through his T-shirt. "Does it hurt?"

"My Darkness stops me from feeling any pain," he replied stiffly.

The playful tone faded from the room and our predicament began to tug at me once more. We had to find the Dark and stop its plot against Camelot, then escape the clutches of both sides of the balance. Then the search for Elijah's cure would begin. My identity problems seemed to be little more than a trifle compared to all of that.

"What will happen to you if we remove your mutation?" I asked. I hadn't thought about the consequences removing his demonic side would have, much like I hadn't thought of my own evolution.

"I don't know…" he admitted. "I might wither and die on the spot, or I may live out the rest of my days as I was meant to."

Watching him closely, I frowned. "You're willing to take the risk?"

"You've seen my mood swings. They're epic." He smirked and held out his hand.

I slipped my palm against his, my shyness forgotten. It didn't matter anymore.

"I can feel you," he murmured.

I shivered, his words sliding over my body. "What is it like?"

"Infinity," he whispered. "I can't see where you end and I begin."

"I don't understand any of it," I admitted as he tugged me onto the bed beside him. "I accepted this without knowing the consequences."

"You didn't have a choice, Madeleine. This is who you are."

"I was made. How can—"

Elijah placed his finger over my lips. "Creation is a fickle concept," he told me. "Your soul has transcended. What came before—your birth, your journey—is irrelevant. Only now exists." He threaded his fingers through mine, locking our hands together.

I thought about the circuit I'd created between my two halves to escape Camelot. Negative to positive. That was inside me, creating an endless loop. I was like an ouroboros serpent eating its own tail, a creature in a constant state of life and death. The paradox of infinity.

"If I have no beginning or end, does that mean…" I took a deep breath to steady my nerves. "Am I immortal?"

Elijah tightened his grip. "I think so."

Now I understood why Wilder was so conflicted about my fate. I hadn't accepted what I'd become yet —not until I allowed my two halves to merge—but he'd seen what I would become when he'd taken my hand.

I was the first—and possibly last—of a new supernatural species and I did not understand how my power worked. I couldn't even fathom how I'd gotten here.

"Do you regret it?" Elijah asked.

I wanted to say yes, but it wasn't entirely true. "It's difficult to let go of a lifetime of belief when you didn't see your fate coming."

"Yes," he said, "it isn't easy."

I looked at him, desperately wanting him to open up to me. Who had he been before? I'd caught a glimpse through the link he'd created between us, but that was it—merely a few images of a life lost.

"That first night below Ben Nevis," I began, "when I touched you… I saw something."

He tensed and I knew he hadn't meant for me to see anything, but neither of us understood what was going on back then. It seemed so long ago, even though it had only been a few short weeks since my capture.

"What did you see?" he asked tentatively.

"An overgrown forest, standing stones, and smoke from a campfire." I worried my bottom lip. "Bare feet dangling in a stream. The rest was blood."

"The day the Dark took me," he murmured.

"When was it?"

He shook his head. "I can't."

"You said they took your colours."

Ramona suspected Elijah hadn't been human and now the pieces seemed to be falling into place. There was only one supernatural race I could think of that manifested their abilities in a prism—a hologram that contained all the colours of the universe.

"Elijah, are you—"

"Madeleine, there's something I need to tell you."

I groaned and let go of his hand, frustrated at his

constant evasion. "Are you kidding? I've had enough secrets and revelations to last a lifetime."

"Unfortunately not." Elijah grimaced and wrung his hands together. "I told you I was only playing at working with the Dark, but that's not entirely true."

"Light help me. I put a lot of faith in you."

"I know, but you took me to Camelot."

"To save your life!" I threw my hands into the air. "And you can't even tell me the truth about yourself!"

"I'm bound to the greater demon who captured you," he blurted.

My blood turned cold and I jerked away from him. "What?"

"That's why I didn't want to go to Camelot."

"What are you saying, Elijah?" I stood and glared at him.

"All I had to do was pass the outer wall," he muttered. "Just stepping foot inside the city was enough."

"Enough for what?"

His gaze met mine. "To let them in."

"It was a set up," I whispered, my eyes widening. "This whole thing was a trick to get back into Camelot."

"Madeleine, no—"

"How dare you!" I screeched, hauling him off the bed and shoving him against the wall. The plaster cracked under the force of the collision and he held up his hands. Grey eyes, unnatural strength…what was I becoming?

"I didn't know," he pleaded.

"I betrayed my people and threw away my entire life for you!"

"Madeleine, I would have gladly died on that hill if I had known they were using me to get to you."

"And now you've killed us both," I snarled. "Why should I let you live? You owe me your life, Elijah."

"That's your Dark talking," he declared. "You wouldn't kill me."

"Yeah? You wanna bet?" I curled my hand around his throat, my power simmering. It appeared within me, swirling like a red and silver oil slick, mixing then separating.

"Not really."

Elijah's power tugged on the invisible tether that bound us. My knees buckled and I collapsed against him with a frustrated cry. His arms wrapped around me, caging my body against his. I struggled for a moment, but his touch was soothing, and I began to settle.

Why was that? I trusted him, I supposed, even though we were still connected. Elijah hadn't let me go, which meant he wasn't afraid of what I was becoming.

That had to mean something.

"I don't know what I am anymore," I whispered, pressing my cheek against his chest. "I feel it inside me, trying to consume everything."

"You know how to control it, Madeleine. You've had a lifetime of training that says you can."

"What am I supposed to do?"

"You're already doing it."

I tensed. "Doing what?"

"Can't you see?" he whispered.

"Your…" My touch had soothed his inner demon.

"Take advantage of it while you can," he drawled.

I didn't know how. My people skills weren't as developed as my warrior abilities.

"What do we do now?" I asked.

"We save your friends," Elijah murmured against my hair. "You fought for the Light your whole life. That doesn't have to change. The rest will come in time."

"If I go back, they'll kill me. Wilder knows what I am. He won't risk me turning to the Dark."

"How do you know? You might turn up when it's most convenient."

"Your demonic duplicity won't work on me."

Elijah snorted and let me go. "Open your mind, Madeleine. It's not about you." I pulled back as if he'd slapped me. "All this time you've been showing me you can handle anything that's thrown at you. What I don't understand is why you can't see it yourself."

I wiped my damp eyes and sat on the end of the bed. It was a little late to deal with my existential crisis right now. I was broken, but so what? Everyone I knew was a little bruised and battered by life. Scarlett was orphaned at three years old when her parents were murdered by the Dark. She'd been ostracised, tormented, and ended up alone in the world until she'd met Jackson and Wilder. Through all the darkness, she'd grown up to become Arondight, one half of the Twin Flames that saved the world. If she could overcome a lifetime of suffering, then so could I.

Camelot was in danger because of me and Elijah. Now I had to get over myself and fix it.

"You're still linked to the Balan?" I asked.

"Yes." Elijah smirked, pleased he'd goaded me into action. Looked as if his demon was showing again.

"Then we sever his hold over you."

"I'm not sure how. I was attempting to use his shackle so I could find you, so I didn't bother trying to remove it. Now it seems like an annoyance more than anything."

"Does he know where you are?"

Elijah shrugged and leaned against the splintered wall. Luckily, we hadn't paid a security deposit on the room because we so weren't getting it back. "Maybe. It's hard to tell. Demons can be so duplicitous."

Choosing to ignore his demonic smart arsery, I said, "The Dark could already be at Camelot. If the Balan is there, we take him out. Death is the easiest way to sever the connection."

"And how do you suppose we kill a greater demon? They're impossible to end, you know."

"Wilder's there," I said, my heartbeat speeding up. "He can kill the Balan. Excalibur has the power."

He grunted and rolled his eyes, his opinion of Excalibur clear. "Or there's the chance that you can."

It was my turn to pout. "I don't know what I can do yet."

"Like I said—"

"Open my mind," I drawled as I stood.

"You can nullify Light, why not the Dark?" His grin widened as his demonic side caught a whiff of imminent chaos. "You can nullify him right out of existence."

I shook my head and shrugged into my jacket. "Whatever. We need to go back to Camelot. If we're lucky, we can warn them the Dark is planning to attack before it's too late."

"I would call it more of an infiltration."

"Elijah."

"So, you want to go back and get ourselves recaptured after we spent all that time escaping?"

I grunted and pulled on my boots. "I'm not arguing about this with you."

He looked me over and wiggled his fingers at me. "You know, when I said take advantage, I meant take *advantage*."

"Seriously?"

Laughing, he opened the door. "Shall we go kill some demons? Chaos is my forte, after all."

18

A full moon had risen over Camelot, casting the entire landscape with a crystallised sheen.

On any other night, I would have thought the iridescent light was beautiful, but when Elijah and I wanted to sneak in the side entrance, it made for terrible cover.

"The sun may as well be out," I muttered as we lingered amongst the ancient stone blocks on the hillside.

"Can't help nature," was Elijah's not-at-all-helpful reply.

Ahead, I could see the entrance to the Natural's base camp just beyond the outer wall. It lay in shadow, the lack of movement alarming.

"Can you sense anything?" I asked, squinting at the horizon where Camelot was even darker.

"Nothing."

"The barrier is gone," I murmured. "There's—"

"Nothing," he quipped. "Just like I said."

Deciding there was nothing we could do by watching further, I ducked out from behind the stone block and made my way towards the camp. We'd find answers there.

It was ironic that I was back after sneaking in and out more times than I could count. Not to mention my grand escape. If I came across a Natural, I'd have to play my cards right or I'd end right back where I had started.

As it turned out, I didn't need to worry. Base camp was dark.

The generators powering the lights and equipment in the infirmary and laboratory tents were silent. Without power, the whole place had fallen into shadows, but that wasn't the only thing out of place. The deeper Elijah and I ventured, the clearer it became that no one was here.

The mess tent had become a ghost town, the stovetops cold and the bain-marie had cooled to icicles. Weirdest of all were the still-full pots on the ovens and the plates of half eaten food on the tables. The barracks and common areas had fared little better. Even the bonfire had simmered to barely-there coals.

It was as if everyone had dropped what they were doing and walked out. There weren't even any tracks, not that I could find any amongst the churned up, muddy ground.

We stood in the centre of camp at a complete loss. How did one hundred Naturals disappear without a trace?

"There's no one here," I said, my heartbeat speeding up. "They're all gone." I glanced at Elijah. "The Naturals would never abandon Camelot. Not even under assault."

"Don't look at me," he said. "They're your people." Well, that was debatable.

"If the Dark has them, then they'll be in Camelot." I pointed up to the shadowy parapets of the castle. "Base camp is useless when what they want is up there."

I moved through the sea of canvas, making a beeline for Thompson's command tent.

"Where are you going?" Elijah asked, trotting after me. "The city's the other way."

"I need to find something first."

I pushed past the flap and looked around the mess of trunks, papers, and racks of miscellaneous weaponry. Thompson really wasn't one for organisation.

Elijah snorted. "Looks like the place was ransacked."

"I don't think so. It always looks like this."

I began to open and close crates, picking up a cold iron dagger to slip into my boot.

He curled his lip and began to poke around the papers on the central table. "How do you people survive?"

I ignored him and picked up a belt, strapping it around my waist. It had pockets and loops for just about everything a Natural warrior would need. All I was missing was my arondight blade.

I glanced at Elijah, but he seemed more interested in the maps and intel stuck to Thompson's whiteboard.

"What are you doing?" I asked.

He looked over his shoulder. "Don't worry. Like any respectable military man would post top-secret patrol routes where anyone could see them." He tapped his finger on the map of the patrol routes and rolled his eyes.

I snorted and continued to search the crates. Until recently, breaking through the Light around the tent hadn't been a problem. Besides, it wasn't like anyone —other than me—could just walk in here and know all our secrets.

Our. Why was it so hard to let go?

I pushed my thoughts aside and kept searching the crates. Time was short and my sword had to be here somewhere. Thompson would want to keep it close so I didn't steal it back.

Ducking under the table he used as a makeshift desk, I found a small black box with an aura of Light around it. Ignoring the magical lock, I clicked open the snaps, my power nullifying the security measures. My transition from warrior to thief was becoming second-nature quicker than I'd expected.

Inside, I saw a glint of metal. *My sword.*

"Yes." I picked up the hilt and held it close.

"I don't know why you want that thing anymore," Elijah said, standing next to me.

"Old habits die hard." I stood and slipped the hilt into my new belt. "Consider it an insurance policy."

Leaving the camp behind, we crossed the wall and ventured into the lower city of Camelot.

We walked through the crumbling streets, moving from building to building with silent footsteps. I placed my hand next to a rune carved into a stone wall—the Druidic rune for the willow tree—and said a silent prayer. So far, nothing had stopped us.

"I've never been here before," Elijah said. "It's a one-star for me."

"One-star?" I scoffed.

"It's in dire need of renovation."

I shook my head and scanned the thoroughfare before us. It was empty, just like the rest of the city and the camp had been.

"Where are all the demons?" I whispered. If this was the Dark taking back Camelot, they were doing a terrible job.

"There aren't many demons left," Elijah told me. "Without a link to the One, all the lower creatures have rotted away. They were the bulk of the horde, you know."

"So, they don't have the numbers for a full scale attack?"

"No. Not unless the scattered come together as one. Without a leader, they'll never have the power they did before the rift closed."

That made our job a little easier, then. I scanned the street and moved towards the main entrance of the inner castle.

Stepping underneath the grand arch at the top of

the thoroughfare, I gasped when I saw what lay beyond.

Naturals were scattered around the square, digging. Some had shovels, others had picks, and some were using their bare hands to move stone and earth. Though the broken gates, I could see more inside the inner bailey doing the same.

I told them to keep digging, but this wasn't what I had in mind.

"What the hell?" Elijah murmured. "This is new."

Sensing no Darkness, I stepped out from under the arch, but no one stopped their work to look at me —they all seemed laser-focused on finding something.

"They're tearing up the place. Aiden's going to be pissed." I cursed and moved across the square, the priceless mosaic ripped up by the dazed Naturals.

"Their eyes are black." I turned to find Elijah squatting in front of a male Natural, his hand wrapped around the man's shovel to stop him from digging. "This one is your friend, isn't he?"

I darted forwards and gasped. "Trent?"

I shook him, but he stared right though me. The moment I let him go, he snatched the shovel from Elijah and kept digging.

"He's zombified," Elijah said. "You won't get any sense out of them. Their eyes are all bugged out."

"What are they doing?" I waved my hand in front of Trent's eyes, but the movement didn't illicit any response.

"Digging."

I glared at Elijah. "Duh."

"I assume whatever the Balan wants, it's buried around here someplace." He walked around a hole another Natural—Maisy—was digging. "He has no chance taking on this many Naturals, so what better way to neutralise the threat than to turn it into a workforce?"

"Then where's Wilder?" I demanded.

"Imprisoned or dead. Take your pick."

I shoved him, my anger getting the better of me. "You're a real arsehole when your demon comes out, you know that?"

He held up his hands. "Don't shoot the messenger, Madeleine."

I sighed and grasped Maisy's arm. Pulling her towards me, I placed both palms on her head and circled my thumbs on her temples. She stared at me with big, black eyes, but didn't stop me.

Reaching for my power, I attempted to connect with her Light. A murky haze lingered inside her mind and I hissed as a jolt of electricity zapped my hands. It'd felt like a slimy film with booby-tapped barbs hidden within the haze.

Letting her go, I cursed. Whatever Darkness held her was beyond my ability to break.

If I knew how this shite worked, then maybe I could free them, but I was clueless. A day in possession of a new soul wasn't exactly enough time to find out my limits.

"It isn't working," I said, turning to Elijah. "I can't break through."

He peered at Maisy, who blinked then returned to her hole. "What did you see?"

"Her mind is full of this awful ashy fog." I shuddered as an echo slunk through my mind.

"I was afraid of that."

"Then how do we break the hypnosis?"

"The Balan is controlling them," he replied. "If we can sever his ritual, then they'll be freed."

"His ritual? Like the sigil he used to get into my mind?"

"Something like that."

I grimaced as I recalled the blood-filled carvings. Why did demons have to be so gross? "Where would we find it?"

"Knowing what he's like, I'd suggest looking outside Camelot."

I hesitated as I looked at the Naturals. I couldn't just leave them here.

"I know what you're thinking, Madeleine," Elijah said, his voice loud in the close quarters of the ruined city. "There's nothing you can do for them. Not until that Balan is six feet under."

He was right, though I didn't let on. He'd never let me live it down.

"High ground," I said. "That's where he'll be."

"A vantage point that gives an unobstructed view of Camelot."

Unobstructed, eh? I had a fair idea where a lookout point like that might be. Trent and I had stood there during our first patrol—the same night the Dark captured me—and we'd argued about the impending doom I felt and his annoyance at my sour attitude. It seemed so long ago, but I knew that's where we'd find the Balan.

"C'mon," I said, "I know where he is."

"See? I knew you'd come along in leaps and bounds when you put your mind to it."

Now that we knew the city was free of demonic invaders, I sprinted through alleys and lanes, vaulting over fallen statues and crumbling walls. Reaching the outer wall, I leapt into the air, using a burst of Light to propel me to the parapet.

Elijah landed next to me and let out a low whistle. "We need to do that more often."

"I'm just glad I haven't lost my edge." I looked out across the Clee Hills and pointed to the rise where Trent and I had stood the night this all began. "There."

Elijah peered over the wall, scoping out the ground below. "Ladies first."

"Coward." I grinned and jumped over the parapet, landing at the bottom on a cushion of Light.

Elijah hit the ground a little heavier but made it in one piece.

"Show off," he said.

"Keep your voice down," I hissed. "Sound carries out here."

We worked our way up the hill together, concealing ourselves as best we could from the bright moonlight. Large stretches of open ground made it difficult, but we climbed the rise without being seen.

It wasn't long before I felt something Dark ahead

of us. Whether it was my newfound abilities making me sensitive, I didn't know, but I was thankful for the early warning system.

I dragged Elijah behind a boulder, lingering out of sight of the demons above.

"Bingo," he said. "Told you so."

I peeked around the edge of the rock. The Balan stood at the top of the rise, flanked by two inky black shadows, bare chested with his arms outstretched. In the crystal moonlight, I could see the blood dripping down his torso, red smeared in a circular pattern over his rotting flesh.

"Is that..." I began, hoping it wasn't what I thought it was.

"A sigil," Elijah confirmed. "Carved into his chest."

I shook my head. "That's seriously messed up."

"It's also a huge problem. That's the ritual we need to stop."

The sigil was linked to the Balan, which meant the only way to sever the bond was to kill him.

"I'll say," I drawled.

"I guess you have to take your new abilities out for a test drive."

I shook my head. "We need Wilder."

"The king hasn't come down from his castle," he drawled. "I'm not relying on Excalibur's arrogance to save us, Madeleine."

"Something's wrong with him because he wouldn't leave Camelot exposed like this."

"We don't have time to go searching for the guy,"

Elijah snapped. "If that Balan finds what he's looking for, we're screwed."

"I don't know how to use my power. What if I choke?"

"You don't have a choice." He held my shoulders. "Madeleine, you're the only one who can get close without falling under the influence of his ritual. It's you or no one."

Some pep talk. I know I'd craved the fight back in London, but now that the stakes were at critical mass I wasn't sure I had the right kind of dreams. Scarlett Ravenwood—Arondight—was my hero and she'd faced far worse. She'd had faith that I'd become a talented Natural, even after I'd mutated. If she could only see me now.

I looked towards the Balan and his twisted ritual. I could do this.

"Well, then," I said to Elijah, "you'd better say here. You're bound to the guy and I don't want you getting in the way."

"You mean you don't want me turning into a zombie."

I smirked and readied my arondight blade. "Something like that."

If this was the first stop on the trail to becoming a better person, then I was about to leap headfirst into the deep end.

I took a deep breath and stepped from behind the boulder.

I didn't want to be late for my date with destiny.

19

———

I climbed the hillside, my gaze fixed on the three demons atop the rise.

The Balan lowered his arms as he sensed my approach, though the flow of Darkness raining over Camelot didn't cease. So much for a stealthy sneak attack.

"Madeleine Greenbriar," he said, turning his black eyes towards me, "I was hoping you'd come."

"I'm getting sick and tired of you sticking your rotted nose where it doesn't belong," I drawled, stopping a few paces away. The sigil hacked into his flesh was even more gruesome than it appeared from far away. "It's time to take out the garbage."

"Is that any way to thank me?" he asked, the stench of blood and rot thick in the air. "I gave you the powers that allowed you to save the life of that snivelling fool, Elijah."

"Demons lie." I laughed and shook my head. "It's in your nature."

"So is death."

The Balan lifted his hand and the two demons flanking him slunk towards me. I struck, my blade exploded into life, the silver sparks twisting with red flame as cold iron sliced through demonic flesh.

The creatures burst into flame, their final deaths consuming their flesh. Heat radiated on either side of me as I focused my gaze onto the Balan.

I was no longer afraid of what I'd become. It fuelled me in a way I'd never felt before and standing before death itself wouldn't stop me from getting what I wanted.

"Are you still using that pathetic toy?" The Balan narrowed his eyes. "*Madeleine.*"

"You keep saying my name like it has power over me, but it just comes off as creepy." I pointed my sword at him. "I'm not like you and I never will be."

"You are *exactly* like me," he snarled. "Naturals may not have a true name, but the demon we made you from does."

"Liar. I don't have a true name."

"Are you sure?"

"Let them go," I hissed through my teeth.

"Not until I get what I want and even then, it will be too late for the Naturals. Camelot belongs to the Dark."

"What do you want with Camelot?" I demanded. "Tell me."

"You'll see." He took a step towards me, congealed blood oozing from the sigil carved into his chest. "We will take this world without our master. We will rise again."

"Not if I have anything to do with it."

I feigned left, then struck right. My sword sliced through the air, falling towards the Balan's ribs.

He ducked and lunged behind me, his bulk moving too fast for me to counter, then slammed his foot down onto the back of my leg.

A scream tore from my lips as jagged bone erupted from my shin. I buckled, falling to the ground in agony.

The Balan stood over me, his eyes black. Glancing at the blood pooling underneath me, he licked his lips, his barbed tongue darting out like a perverted lizard tasting the air.

"Pathetic," he said, lowering himself over me. "You don't even understand the gift the Dark has given you."

I grimaced as I tried to wriggle away from the rotting creature, but his hands slammed down beside my head, caging me within his grasp.

"We would have been unstoppable," he rasped, curling a clammy hand around my throat. "You would have been my queen."

"Gross," I choked out. "You reek of rotting flesh. Haven't you heard of deodorant? It's common courtesy."

The Balan snarled and tightened his grip. "You accepted your fate. Now embrace it."

White-hot barbs dug into my mind and I screamed as the demon began to drill into my head.

Without the focused power of his sigil, the invasion was agonising.

"You can't control me," I cried, fighting the power that was clawing inside me.

"You would fight for them?" His rotting breath stank as the creature bared its rows of razor-sharp teeth. "They tortured you for years, blaming you for their own shortcomings. They will execute you. The Dark will embrace you, Madeleine. Come with me and I will show you just how powerful you really are. I would never hold you back. With me, you can be free."

I gasped as images began to flash through my mind. Freedom. Acceptance. Meaning. All the things I'd dreamed of…

"No!" I screeched. "I don't believe you!"

"All you have to do is let go. Let go and you can have everything you have ever wanted."

The Balan was torn away from me, the connection between our minds severed. I roared as his barbs dragged through my psyche, but I was free.

I opened my eyes to find a familiar form standing over me. *Elijah.*

"What are you doing?" I dragged myself to my knees, my broken leg dangling uselessly. "You can't be here!"

He shoved me aside as he passed, not even looking at me. His hand brushed against my bare skin and I froze as cold Darkness rushed through our connection. Everything that made him human was gone.

I cried out as I felt the link between us sever. "Elijah, *no…*"

But he wasn't paying any attention to me. His gaze was focused solely on the Balan. What could he possibly do to the demon who had bound his soul? Nothing, unless he didn't have one.

No… The gravity of what he'd just done slammed into me and I almost collapsed. Elijah had severed the connection with his soul and now he was one hundred percent Dark—he'd given up his freedom to save me.

His voice echoed across the hillside. "Ikakantor, your time has come."

The Balan demon roared and fell to his knees as if an invisible force pushed him.

Ikakantor? It must be his true name. Elijah had just levelled the playing field.

"You have no power over me anymore," he said as he stood over the demon.

"You waited this long to play your hand?" Ikakantor asked with a sneer. "What is it about her?"

Silver glinted in Elijah's hand—my arondight hilt. "I guess you'll never know."

Electric sparks showered across the trail as the blade erupted, links of cold iron clicking together as he swung.

The blade sliced through the Balan's neck, severing his head from his shoulders. A black, inky cloud poured out of the hacked flesh, rushing into the air. It pooled in the sky like an angry storm cloud, crackling with menacing Darkness.

The empty body slumped to the ground and

exploded into flame, the fireball consuming flesh until there was nothing left but a scorch mark on the grass.

The Balan was an inky mass of swirling energy raging above us. Without another body to possess, it was powerless against us. It began to rise, flying away from us and Camelot until it disappeared into the night.

Elijah let my sword retract and knelt beside me.

"My sword. How…?"

"Shh," he murmured, evading my question yet again. "I've got to set your leg. I doubt your fancy doctor could set a break like that without causing some damage."

"And you can?"

"Let's find out." He smirked and set the hilt beside me. "I will need two hands for this."

"What—"

He pressed down on my shin and I screamed a perverse curse as the bone crunched back into place.

"Seriously?" I exclaimed, punching him in the arm.

"I think the words you're looking for are 'thank you'." Looking at the wound in my leg, he added, "Give it a minute and you'll be fine."

"I think I'll need a lot longer than that."

"I doubt it." He winked. "You've got the best of both worlds now."

I grasped his wrist. "Did you have to?"

"It was clear you were losing," he replied. "It wasn't a clean kill, but at least you're free."

"You gave up the last connection to your soul to save my life. Why?"

He lowered his gaze, hiding their silver sheen from me. "Don't read too much into it."

Leaving me, Elijah walked over to the scorched ground where Ikakantor had made his last stand and scuffed his toe across the soot. The Balan's body was gone, but I knew he had more hanging in his meat closet—unless the team of Naturals the Regula had sent had evicted him from Ben Nevis. Even so, the Balan would be back but not any time soon. A small win, but I would take whatever I could get.

I sat, the pain in my leg subsiding to a dull throb and picked up my arondight blade. More questions and even fewer answers. Elijah could wield my sword, yet he wasn't a Natural. That only left one thing he could be, but even if I asked, he'd never admit to it. His people had left after the cataclysm over eight hundred years ago and none remained. If I was right, it also meant he'd walked the Earth for far longer than any creature, besides the immortal greater demons.

He could avoid my questioning all he wanted, but I would continue to believe that Elijah was once a Druid.

What that meant for his cure now that he'd given up his soul was anyone's guess.

When I rose, it surprised me to find he was right about my body's accelerated healing. Apart from the blood and the tear in my jeggings, it was as if I had never broken my leg.

Yet another mystery.

I stood before him, knowing his demon side was in control. His lip curved upwards and I knew I was about to cop a mouthful of curse-laden sass. The sweet Elijah who'd given me my first kiss and tried to convince me to run away with him was dormant. The longer I studied the silver eyes staring down at me, the more I understood that I might not see that part of him again.

"Ikakantor?" I asked, tilting my head to the side.

"Names have power," he replied with a smirk. "If you know a demon's true name, you can bring it to its knees." I had to remember that for when he came back.

"I assume Elijah isn't yours anymore."

"Elijah's still here," he told me, fostering a small spark of hope. "And we have the same agenda…for now."

"And that is?"

"Freedom," he replied simply. "What's the one thing stopping the Dark from regaining a foothold in this world?"

I stared at him, dread rising in my gut. "The Twin Flames."

Elijah nodded and looked towards Camelot. "I don't know what they're looking for, but now we know for sure it's in the city. Warn them if you can."

"If they take me back."

"Of course, they will. After what you did for them, they'd be stupid not to."

"You mean after what *you* did."

Elijah grinned and winked. "I won't tell if you don't."

I reached out and took his hand. Maybe I could bring him back…

"That won't work anymore," he told me.

"It was worth a try."

"You've seen too much, you know."

"If I could rub bleach into my eyes to get the stain out, I would," I said with a snort. "Meat closets, self-mutilation, and bug-eyed zombies are enough to turn anyone off. Besides, killing me won't help you."

"I'm not sure I can kill you."

"That too."

"You're like me," he said as he fingered a strand of my hair. "But you're also like them."

"I could go either way, you know."

"You feel too much to become Dark," he told me. "No… I think your truth isn't as clear as that."

I felt the ghost of his kiss on my lips, his assessment revealing the reality of his choice. "You can't love anymore, can you?"

He shrugged, indifferent. "I have a human-ish heart. What I can do with it remains to be seen."

I lowered my gaze, feeling the loss of our bond deeper than I thought I would.

"Don't be disappointed. He did this for you," he told me.

"Knowing doesn't make it any easier. I would've liked to have you with me for this next part. I'll have to go down that hill and explain myself."

Elijah studied me, his gaze cold. If I didn't know

the truth of what he was, I would have pulled away…
but I didn't.

"Who do you choose, Madeleine?" His voice was
hushed, though the wind carried it towards me.

"This goes beyond good and evil—Light and
Dark," I replied. "I choose neither. I'm declaring for
life."

His lips curved into a lopsided grin. "Pretty
Spectre."

"Did you just make that up?"

"Clever, aren't I?"

"Careful, your demon is showing."

Elijah laughed and turned towards Camelot. He
and I knew this was just the beginning of
something far greater than he and I had already
faced.

"I'm sorry I couldn't help you find your cure," I
said softly.

"It's okay," he told me. "I made peace with who
I'd become a long time ago."

"And now you're leaving."

"I have to. After all…I'm the enemy."

"Dammit, and I was just beginning to like you," I
said, tilting my head to the side.

His lips quirked. "Don't lie. We both know you
liked me from the beginning."

"How are you so sure?"

"Every time you thought about me—"

"You felt a little tug." I smirked and shook my
head. "Men are all the same."

He tilted his head to the side. "Are they?" He

tucked my hair behind my ear, his fingers brushing against my cheek.

My heart did a backflip. "Will I ever see you again?"

"Maybe," he replied. "You walk in both worlds now."

"Can you stay a while longer?"

His lips curved and he nodded. "Maybe just for a moment."

Together, we watched the sun rise over the ruined parapets of Camelot, the cusp of a new future laid before us. After last night, the world had changed irrevocably. The cataclysm, the eight hundred year war, the Dark Night, the final battle to close the rift… all of it had led to this moment. Now the Dark's last stand was upon us.

I just hoped I had the strength to face it.

20

Dawn still hadn't reached within Camelot's walls by the time I made it back to the city.

The Naturals had made their way back to base camp, shuffling through the after-effects of their zombified states. No one noticed me as I walked through the tents, searching for a familiar and friendly face. They were all too dazed to notice a wanted fugitive.

I spotted Trent and Maisy by the bonfire. They were covered with dirt and grime and talked intently to one another. The glow of the fire radiated behind them, staving off the chill.

What was I supposed to say to them? An apology wasn't going to be enough to fix the trouble I'd caused.

Sensing my presence, they looked up.

"Madeleine!" Maisy rose to her feet in shock and Trent's dazed expression turned to a serious frown.

I stopped a few paces away, unsure.

Maisy ran at me and threw her arms around my neck. "When Trent told me you'd… I didn't believe it."

Heaving a sigh of relief, I glanced at Trent over her shoulder and he shrugged.

"There was a Balan demon on the hill," I explained. "The same one who took me."

Trent's frown deepened.

"He was controlling everyone with some weird sigil carved into his chest," I went on. "I had to kill him to sever the connection."

Trent shook his head and grinned. "I knew I was right about you."

Maisy pulled back and stared at me like the sun shone out of my rear end. "Wait… You killed a greater demon?"

"Just his body," I said, the lie weighing heavily on my heart. "He'll be back."

"Still, that's some serious shite, Mads," Trent told me.

I let Maisy go and wiped away her tears. "I need to find Aiden and do some explaining. Have you seen him?"

"I heard he was at the castle looking for the Inquisitor," she told me.

I frowned, another wave of dread rising. And here I was thinking it was all over. "Wilder still hasn't come back?"

"No one's seen him since he spoke to you," Trent

confirmed. "He went up to the castle and never came back."

"Shite." I turned towards Camelot.

"Madeleine?"

I hesitated at the sound of Maisy's voice. "Yeah?"

"Are you back? I mean, are you…?"

"I'm not Dark," I told them. "I'm…in between."

There was nothing else I could explain, so I left them beside the warmth of the fire and returned to the city.

It was time to face the music.

***

I found Aiden inside the castle grounds. From here, I could see the rift in all its terrifying glory. The chasm opened before me, the pit so deep the bottom hid in shadow.

Camelot itself was a massive structure, its tallest tower maybe fifteen stories high, and the surrounding walls and grounds as large as the one-hundred-and-forty-hectare Hyde Park in London.

Once, it had likely been filled with lush gardens, pavilions, busy stables, bustling kitchens, and more. Now it was torn in half, its towers crumbling, its stone charred black, and dust and ash as far as the eye could see. Not even the passage of time had allowed nature to reclaim this place from the Dark.

Camelot was dead.

Turning my back on the chasm, I approached

another pit. This one was fresher, having been dug during the night and all.

Aiden stood at the bottom, his hands pressed against the wall of a hidden structure just like the one he'd unearthed weeks before. From the wave of energy radiating from it, I assumed they were linked, except this time I didn't feel sick. The energy seemed to harmonise within me, drawing me closer.

I skidded down the side of the hole and landed beside Aiden. He looked up at me, startled by my sudden appearance.

He blinked. "Madeleine?"

"Don't look so surprised." I held out my hand. "Let's get you out of this hole, huh?"

Aiden coughed, dust and grit falling from his hair, and he grasped my hand. As our skin touched, his gaze flew to mine.

"Don't give me that look," I told him. "I'll explain later."

"What happened?"

"There was a greater demon controlling you," I replied. "The same Balan who took me."

"A Balan demon in Camelot?"

"I killed his body to sever the ritual. It was the only way to free you."

"What a predicament." He scratched his head. "Considering the chaos you've caused, I should probably arrest you or something."

"I hope not," I drawled. "I went to a lot of trouble to come back here."

"Madeleine…you're a hybrid now. That makes you unpredictable."

"I'm only unpredictable because the Light doesn't understand me, let alone how to control me with its list of Codex regulations." I sighed and placed my hands on his shoulders. "You can feel what's inside me, Aiden, and now I know who I'm supposed to be. I could have left and never returned, but here I am."

"Light help me," he muttered.

"Do you know that silver and red make pink?"

Aiden blinked in bewilderment. "Your Light is pink?"

"Kind of." I made a face. "You know, I loathe pink."

The air between us eased somewhat and I helped him scramble out of the hole he'd dug—pardon the pun.

"It was the strangest thing," he murmured. "The last thing I remember was going to bed. Then I woke up in a ditch with a shovel in my hands."

"Well, we knew the Dark was looking for something in Camelot."

He tugged me towards another hole, this one closer to the rift. "I wonder…"

We stood on the edge of the crater, the wind whipping at our backs. The first rays of dawn had finally edged their way over the lip and fell upon the border of runes.

"It's the entrance to an archive," Aiden told me. "A repository of information and relics which date back thousands of years."

My heart skipped a beat and I knew we'd just dodged a whole spray of bullets. Aiden believed it held the culmination of Camelot's power.

A set of large, metallic double doors were set into the wall, etched with elaborate carvings. Aiden had disturbed the ground where he'd pushed his way in, but the rest looked as if it had just seen the light of day for the first time in centuries.

"After I woke, I went inside," Aiden continued, stating the obvious. "And from what I can tell, it remains untouched by the Dark."

"You know what this means, right?" I asked. "What they want is probably in there."

"Come inside and see for yourself."

Aiden held up his hand and melded a spark of Light into a small, round ball. Letting it go, it hovered between us, lighting our path into the archive.

We ducked through the opening and descended a flight of stairs. Rows of shelving reaching to the ceiling were crammed into the first room. Books and scrolls lay everywhere, covered in dust and cobwebs. Doors opened into more rooms, each filled with ancient pottery, statues, talismans, weapons, and jewels. It was a treasure trove of lost knowledge.

"It's huge," I whispered, my voice echoing all around us.

"There are doors and passages that cut into the hillside," Aiden said excitedly. "And stairs going farther down."

I slapped my palm against my forehead. "Don't tell me you already went down."

"All the way to the bottom."

"You want me to go down there with you, don't you?"

"Uh-huh."

I groaned.

"You said you could help us find Darkness here," he said. "Can you?"

"I guess, but—"

"Great." He grabbed my arm and dragged me through the mysterious archive, not in the least bit concerned about magical traps and other creepy crawlies that might lurk in the dark.

The air cooled as we worked our way into the earth, passing untold treasures. Aiden had found something at the end of the archive that worried him enough that he needed me to verify its origin.

The last flight of stairs led to a long passageway and at the end, another set of doors similar to those outside. These were a little more fortified—gears and strange mechanisms were inlaid in the copper and gold façade—and when locks were on doors, it could only mean one thing. Treasure.

We stared at the door, neither of us knowing what to say, let alone do.

"That's a problem," Aiden stated, his voice quivering.

"What are you talking about?" I asked. "It's a door."

"Can't you feel it?" He pointed to the lock. "I haven't felt that kind of power since—"

"The Twin Flames," I finished as the same power washed over me.

"And it's behind a locked door. Madeleine...that's a vault."

Then the million-dollar question was, what was inside? There must have been thousands of relics hidden in here, but the most logical explanation for the Dark's digging had to be this. No one locked something deep underground if it wasn't powerful and dangerous to boot.

I pressed my palm against the door. The metal was cool to the touch, but warmth ebbed from within and I snatched my hand away.

"Light," I whispered.

"Light?" He inspected the carvings but didn't move to touch like I had.

"Aiden, the Twin Flames turned out to be people, not swords," I said. "What if it's a prison?"

"A prison?" He contemplated my theory. "The Dark held Camelot for centuries..."

"What if they caught something?" My heart skipped a beat. "What if the Naturals caught something?" The only other creature we knew who held the same kind of power was the one who'd given it in the first place. "What if it's the Lady of the Lake?"

"No," Aiden replied. "Scarlett said she locked herself inside Avalon after the timeline changed. This can't be her."

I swallowed hard. "Then it's something else."

"Whatever it is, we have to protect this place."

"We need Wilder," I said. "Trent and Maisy said he hasn't come back from the castle. Well, we're at the castle…"

Shuffling footsteps echoed behind us and we spun. I reached for my arondight blade just as Wilder appeared inside Aiden's halo of Light.

"Wilder, I—" I hesitated when I saw the sheen of sweat beading across his forehead.

He stumbled and leaned against the wall, his breath rattling in his lungs.

"He's sick," Aiden said, frozen. "The Flames shouldn't get sick."

"Madeleine," Wilder rasped and I went to meet him, "can you…"

I held his hands and gasped as my newfound power reached out towards him. His Flame was dimming.

"Scarlett…" he rasped, collapsing against the wall. "I need Arondight."

I looked to Aiden, my heartbeat speeding up. "What's wrong with him?"

"Madeleine. Let him go."

I snatched my hands away and Wilder slid down the wall, gasping for breath. Aiden thought I was draining his power.

"No," I said, shaking my head. "It isn't me. Aiden—"

"Stand back," he ordered, edging himself between me and Wilder. "I can't take that chance."

"I'm not that powerful!" I exclaimed. "I can't dim a Flame!"

"We don't understand what you've become." He shook his head and knelt beside Wilder, who'd fallen into incoherency. "I'm sorry, Madeleine, but I will have to lock you up after all."

"No." I shook my head and backed away. "I won't go back into that cage."

"It's for your own safety."

"Yours, you mean." I jabbed a finger at the vault door. "It's that thing that's making him sick. Don't you think it's a coincidence? The Naturals lock it away, the Dark wants to dig it up, and now Wilder's sick?"

He hesitated, glancing at the Inquisitor.

"Aiden," I snapped, "we need to get him to Ramona."

He blinked and rose to his feet, snapping to attention. "Help me get him up."

Together, we lifted Wilder and began the long trek to the surface. I could sense Excalibur waning, his silver Flame dimming like a candle in the wind. Whatever was in that vault, didn't bode well.

"Straight to the infirmary," Aiden reminded me.

I just hoped we got there in time.

We dragged Wilder through base camp, picking up a trail of bewildered Naturals as we went. They lingered outside as we burst into the infirmary.

Ramona stared at us, her mouth falling open. "Madeleine? What—"

"He's sick," I interrupted, helping Aiden lay Wilder on bed. "His Flame is dimming."

She snapped to attention and leaned over him, administering her Light. Her eyes fluttered closed as she ran her hands over his head and chest. She went so deep into his mind I wondered if she would ever come out.

"Ramona?" Aiden urged. "What's happening to him?"

She lifted her hands and shook her head, distraught.

"Ramona?" I murmured, laying a hand on her shoulder.

Her gaze met mine, disbelief clear in her eyes. "He's in a coma."

"A coma? How is that possible?"

Aiden sucked in a sharp breath. "But he's Excalibur. He can't——"

"It's that stupid vault!" I exclaimed, my power sparking. "And that bloody Balan, Ikakantor. *I'll kill him.*"

I went for my arondight blade, but Ramona grasped my wrist. "*Madeleine.*"

"Holy…" Aiden stared at me.

"What?" I demanded. "While we stand here like morons, Wilder is slipping further away. Where's Scarlett? We need to——"

"Madeleine," Ramona said, "calm yourself."

I tensed as Aiden handed me the tablet. Looking at the screen, I saw the screen was open to the camera. My image stared back at me, angry and otherworldly. I gasped and dropped the tablet. My eyes were black and thin veins had spread outwards across my face like a morbid mask.

"We have to report this to the Regula," Ramona said to me. "All of it. We're dealing with things we don't understand."

I drew in breath after breath, my heart speeding up. "What's happening to me?"

"We don't know." Aiden stood beside me, his expression full of worry. "But we'll figure it out. Together, okay?"

I needed Wilder and Scarlett. I needed my family and friends. Most of all, I needed Elijah, but he was gone. He had faith in me, challenged me to open my mind, and forced me to see the strength I was capable of. It was time to accept what he'd been trying to beat into my stupid head and run with it.

"I know I've disappointed you," I told them. "I just hope I can live long enough to make it up to everyone."

"Madeleine, you saved us," Ramona said. "That's all the proof I need of your allegiance. The Regula will see reason."

"Ditto," Aiden said.

I looked to Wilder. His skin had taken on a greyish hue, his breathing shallow.

"Screw the Regula," I said. "Now, we save Excalibur."

Madeleine's adventure continues with DEMON SWORN, the second book in The Camelot Archive!

A buried secret and a goth girl with a massive attitude. The bad guys don't stand a chance.

Keep reading to the end of this ebook for an exclusive peek at the next chapter...

ABOUT NICOLE

Nicole R. Taylor is an Australian Urban Fantasy author.

She lives in the western suburbs of Melbourne dreaming up nail biting stories featuring sassy witches, duplicitous vampires, hunky shapeshifters, and devious monsters.

She likes chocolate, cat memes, and video games.

When she's not writing, she likes to think of what she's writing next.

Follow Nicole Online:

Website: www.nicolertaylorwrites.com
Facebook: facebook.com/nrtaylorwrites
Newsletter: www.nicolertaylorwrites.com/newsletter
Email: nicole.this.is@gmail.com

DEMON SWORN (THE CAMELOT ARCHIVE - BOOK TWO)

CHAPTER ONE

London was busier than I remembered.

I'd been at Camelot for a month, but it felt like an eternity after everything I'd been through. The city was crowded, buildings pressed in on me, and it was full of pollution. After spending my whole life dreaming of being stationed here after my training, it was ironic that I was longing for the countryside. Stillness and stars were foreign concepts here.

I sat inside the London Sanctum, the headquarters of the Naturals—the demon-hunting mages who protected the Earth from the Darkness beyond—awaiting the ultimate question time.

The hall was empty, though I could hear the murmuring of voices through the carved double doors in front of me—and they didn't sound happy.

I shuffled my boots over the marble floor tiles, studying the pattern of black and grey as it splintered through white stone. Anything to keep my mind focused.

In the last month, I'd broken just about every rule, regulation, and covenant laid out in the Codex. The humans had their various religions with their sacred texts, and the Naturals had theirs in the Codex. No one was exempt from a higher power, though we knew for sure ours existed. The Lady of the Lake, a celestial being of unknown origins who'd gifted the first Naturals with their power and had given us Excalibur and Arondight.

"Madeleine Greenbriar."

My heart leapt and I looked up to find a familiar face staring down at me. A tall, gangly man with messy brown hair and a rumpled T-shirt with the slogan 'keep calm and respawn' on the front grinned down at me. I assumed the writing on the shirt was a video game reference—he was a professional gamer before joining the Sanctum—but it went straight over my head.

"Jackson?"

"Hey," he replied and sat beside me. "I can't say I'm surprised, but that's a nice jacket. It goes especially well with the combat boots."

"Still hilarious, I see."

He grinned and leaned against the wall. Jackson was the human best friend of Arondight—otherwise known as Scarlett Ravenwood—and had once been like me. As a victim of Human Convergence, he was mutated with demonic genes through possession. He'd been cured after the death of Mordred—the twisted

Natural the Dark had synthesised the infection from —and was now one hundred percent human.

"How's Esme?" Esme was his wife and fellow Human Convergence survivor.

"Great," he replied. "She's heading up the infirmary while Ramona is at Camelot."

"And how are your inventions coming along? Built anything yet?"

"I'm working on a device to detect demonic possession," he told me. "It's to do with particle waves and quantum physics. I know you're supposed to be able to do that stuff now, but we're not as lucky."

"I didn't ask for this, you know."

He frowned. "Yeah, I know. I don't think anyone saw this coming when Scarlett saved your soul."

"I'm glad she did, though. Being wiped from existence would have sucked."

Jackson nodded towards the assembly. "What are you going to tell them?"

That was the question of the day. The enemy had captured me, I'd been imprisoned by my own people —twice—escaped both times, constantly defied orders, and teamed up with a demon to save Camelot. Most of those things were punishable by exile, even with the stripping of Light—the power that made a Natural who they were—but I wasn't exactly the same person I was when I'd been demoted to guard duty at the archeological site of Camelot.

The greater demon, Ikakantor, had awoken the dormant demonic mutation lodged in my soul, intending to use me to uncover some secret buried below the castle. After being forced to accept who I was becoming to save my friends, I was now half Light and half Dark.

And what that meant exactly was anyone's guess, least of all mine.

Then there was Elijah…

"I don't know," I said, finally replying to Jackson's question.

"The truth always helps," he commented as he glanced past me. "What happened to Wilder wasn't your fault."

Following his gaze, I noted the guards stationed at the end of the hall. Looking in the other direction, two more men stood by the double doors leading out to the main foyer of the Sanctum.

They trusted me…to a point. It wouldn't take any effort for me to walk out of here. I wouldn't even have to raise a hand. Being a part of both worlds, I could nullify the powers of both. I hadn't tried the Dark yet and had failed miserably when I'd tried, but I understood Light and getting past it was easy. Training your whole life to become a warrior was good for times like these, though it was terrible for building trust.

"Madeleine."

I looked up at the Natural down the hall. The tall man I didn't recognise was a representative from the Regula, the governing body of the Naturals.

"They're ready for you."

I nodded and rose to my feet, smoothing down my black suit jacket. First impressions counted, especially when you were accused of consorting with the enemy.

"Good luck," Jackson said, rising with me. "Remember—"

"Jackson." I pouted and brushed him off.

"I know, but my fickle human heart wants to say it out loud."

I attempted a smile, but I was entirely positive it looked like a twisted grimace. Turning towards the doors, I pushed them open and strode inside. Better to get this over and done with as soon as possible.

The gallery was a large round room with a domed skylight. Tiered seating surrounded the entire space, climbing five levels. Eight hundred Naturals could cram themselves in here, but only one hundred were stationed in London at any one time. They weren't all warriors, but support personnel like scientists, doctors, cooks, trainers, researchers, and assistants. Of that number, less than half patrolled the city, protecting its people against demonic possession.

I supposed that's why everyone took things so seriously around here. The loss of one was the loss of many.

I stood in the centre of the gallery, illuminated in a circle of overcast light filtering through the dome, and looked up at the representatives sent by the Regula. Wilder was the Inquisitor—the Naturals' version of a Prime Minister—but ever since he'd fallen into a coma—which was another reason I was here—Greer had taken his place.

Greer was the protector of the Codex. Selected by

fate and powers beyond reasoning, she alone was tasked with keeping the powerful book safe, recounting its lessons and adding new pages. If an unworthy touched it, they'd burn from the inside out. It was one hell of a firewall, *pun intended.*

She could be sweet with her angelic face, blemish free skin, shiny almond-coloured hair, and perfect wardrobe, but her wrath was terrible.

To her right sat Aldrich, Scarlett's uncle and long-time council member at the London Sanctum. He now served as part of the Regula beside the Inquisitor. Grey-haired and weathered by decades fighting on the front lines, he was wise, calm, and the fatherly figure everyone wish they had.

To her left was a man I didn't recognise and to my annoyance, no one bothered to introduce him. He looked a little young to be sitting beside such esteemed Naturals, but I wasn't in the position to question the authority of our government. They assured me I wasn't on trial, but it sure felt like it.

I could tell the new guy was handsome, but he wasn't my type. He was clean cut and impeccably dressed in a tailored black suit jacket and crisp navy shirt. His sharp green eyes stared at me like I was transparent. His caramel-coloured hair even had that artful swoosh that was meticulously styled to look like he rolled out of bed that way. Even so, I wasn't blind. He was good-looking, but I usually went for men with darker colouring and who were a little rugged around the edges—like Elijah.

My heart twisted at the thought of him. The last

time I'd seen the half-demon, he'd given in to his Dark side, cut Ikakantor's head off to save Camelot, then told me to take all the credit so I could keep my place amongst the Naturals. Who knew where he was now?

"Madeleine Greenbriar, you stand here accused of treason, assault, and conspiracy," Greer said, her voice echoing through the chamber. "Among other things."

"You conspired to flee with a demon," Aldrich said. "Why?"

I cleared my throat. "He freed me from a greater demon's lair. In exchange, all he wanted was help with finding a cure—"

"A cure you couldn't give," the unknown man stated. He even sounded posh.

"No, but—"

"And why was that?" he pressed, cutting me off yet again.

"Because Ramona found he wasn't mutated like I had been. He was different."

"Different how?" Greer asked.

"She never got the time to find that out," I replied.

"Because you broke out of your bonds and helped him escape," the man snapped.

"I left because no one believed my intentions or Elijah's were good," I said, my voice rising. "You're all too hung up on the fact that I have some bad guy's DNA to see the threat growing on our doorstep. If I hadn't broken out and stopped Ikakantor, the Dark would have used the Naturals to finish digging up Camelot and this conversation we're having would be very different."

"What is the Dark looking for?" he demanded.

I rolled my eyes. "How would I know?"

"You're connected to the Dark. You tell me."

"Careful," I hissed, "your prejudice is showing."

"Enough," Greer snapped, slamming her fist down onto the table.

"Madeleine, you obviously have some strong opinions," Aldrich urged, his voice a welcome calm amongst the rising tension. "Tell us what you would do."

"You shouldn't be so hung up on following the law as it was written in an eight hundred-year-old book," I told them. "The Codex was created in a world under threat from the demonic creatures beyond the rift. Now the rift is closed and the Dark which remains isn't the same enemy. The Light must evolve just as the Dark has or it will perish. The future is here, and it is in jeopardy. We can't rely on archaic beliefs to save the world from an evolving threat."

"They'd be wise words if they weren't coming from a hybrid," the man spat. "A hybrid who can nullify Light and do whatever the hell she wants."

"*Issac*," Greer snapped, "we do not judge with hostility within these walls."

"She said it herself," the man known as Issac argued. "We can't rely on *archaic beliefs*."

"There is a shred of truth in her words," Aldrich

said. "It is folly to remain still when the enemy is speeding up."

"Perhaps," Issac shook his head, "but she accepted her soul and merged her powers the same night a greater demon attacked Camelot and the Twin Flames fell into a coma."

"Scarlett was nowhere near Camelot," Aldrich told him.

"It doesn't matter," Issac countered. "The Twin Flames are linked. If one falls, they both suffer."

My heart plummeted. "Scarlett's sick?" *Why didn't Jackson tell me?*

Greer sighed and nodded. "Whatever ailment has taken Wilder has also affected Scarlett."

"Where is she? Can I—"

Issac snorted. "Do you really think we would let you anywhere near the Flames?"

"She saved my life!" I exclaimed, my voice echoing around the gallery. "Why would I wish this on her?"

"Because when she saved your life, your soul came back along with the Darkness that infected you," Issac told me. "It isn't beyond reason you'd harbour ill will towards her for that."

"No! You're putting words in my mouth."

Greer rose to her feet, cutting Issac off. *"Enough."* Her gaze found mine and I thought I saw a shred of pity in them. "You slew Ikakantor and broke his hold over the Naturals at Camelot," she continued. "However, you attacked a fellow Natural, escaped confinement not once but twice, and conspired to free a demon who is now unaccounted for. Do you deny it?"

I jutted out my chin. "No, I do not."

"Where is the demon Elijah?" she pressed.

"Hybrid," I corrected. "He was mutated. Ramona has the evidence."

She nodded, her lips thin. "Where is the hybrid?"

"I don't know."

"Convenient," Issac spat.

"He left after I slew Ikakantor's body, fearing he'd be cut open and experimented on," I said, seething. "And I don't blame him. I will make it a point that if it wasn't for Elijah, we wouldn't know the Balan demon's true name."

"She's sympathetic to them," Issac hissed at the others. "What's stopping her from turning against us? If she goes Dark, we can't do anything."

Greer turned to face him, her eyes narrowing. "You," she said evenly. "You're stopping her."

"Excuse me?" he and I blurted it at the same time, looking at each other with open dislike.

"It's clear your newfound abilities require further study," she went on. "And that they are linked to your emotions. I do not doubt your intentions, Madeleine, but we all understand how emotions can get the better of us. We do have a human element to our species, after all."

"You believe me?" I asked, my mouth falling open.

"I believe you had no part in the sickness that overcame Wilder. Aiden Thompson mentioned the vault in Camelot's archive was emitting a strange power that may have something to do with it, and the timing was within range. *However...* more study is needed and my benevolence towards your multiple insurrections comes with certain conditions."

I nodded, lowering my gaze. It was wishful thinking to hope that I'd walk out of here without some kind of punishment, but at least Greer seemed to be leaning towards not throwing me into prison in the Glastonbury catacombs. That place was dark, wet, and miserable.

"You will return to Camelot and assist Aiden with the cataloging of the archive. Your abilities may be a welcome benefit for his continued studies. This was his request, so do not disappoint him a third time. While not in his service, you will report to Issac once daily for training. He will assist you with controlling and developing your abilities."

"Impossible," he complained.

Greer turned her glare onto Issac. "This is not negotiable. It's a direct order, Issac." To me, she added yet another condition, "You must understand your new reality, Madeleine, and earn the Naturals' trust back."

"The Naturals?" I narrowed my eyes. "So, I'm no longer seen as one of you?"

She didn't honour me with a response, just the ultimate full stop. "And you must inform us immediately if the demon-hybrid Elijah contacts you, otherwise we will have no choice but to confine you. Am I clear?"

My jaw tightened and I stood tall. There was no way I was going to let Issac see a single shred of weakness in me. He was determined to see me fail, I was sure of it.

"Yes," I said, "I understand."

"Then you will return to Camelot this evening." Greer nodded and gestured towards the doors. "Dismissed."

I shot Issac one last glare, salty over the fact that I'd have to share a car with him for the three hours back to base camp. Cataloguing dusty scrolls and pottery, and daily training with the ultimate prejudiced arsehole was going to wear thin, real quick. I wasn't born yesterday.

I'd just been given a babysitter.

***

Demon Sworn is OUT NOW!

Druids, witches, fae, and shapeshifters abound in this thrilling magical adventure!

Find out more at: NicoleRTaylorWrites.com

See what titles are FREE at: Nicole's Free Reads